Jenna's heart skipped a scheduled beat as a pair of amber eyes locked on her.

At some point in the past twelve hours, a startling transformation had occurred. The heavy growth of stubble that had shadowed Dev's face had been removed, enhancing the clean lines of his chiseled features.

In faded jeans and a dark green T-shirt that accentuated broad shoulders and muscular arms, Dev looked like a man totally at ease in his surroundings.

And way too attractive for her peace of mind.

Jenna stopped.

"Do you need some help?"

He'd noticed the heel of her shoe stuck in the sand.

"I'm—"

"Fine," Dev interrupted. "I think you made that clear yesterday. But at the moment it looks like you're…stuck."

A large hand curved around her ankle. The unexpected touch caught Jenna off guard. And sent an equally unexpected jolt of electricity running through her.

"If you're going to stick around for a while, you should think about getting something a little more…" With another small tug, Dev set her free. "Practical."

Books by Kathryn Springer

Love Inspired

Tested by Fire
Her Christmas Wish
By Her Side
For Her Son's Love
A Treasure Worth Keeping
Hidden Treasures
Family Treasures
Jingle Bell Babies
*A Place to Call Home
*Love Finds a Home
*The Prodigal Comes Home
The Prodigal's Christmas Reunion
*Longing for Home
*The Promise of Home

*Mirror Lake

Steeple Hill Books

Front Porch Princess
Hearts Evergreen
    "A Match Made for Christmas"
Picket Fence Promises
The Prince Charming List

KATHRYN SPRINGER

is a lifelong Wisconsin resident. Growing up in a "newspaper" family, she spent long hours as a child plunking out stories on her mother's typewriter and hasn't stopped writing since! She loves to write inspirational romance because it allows her to combine her faith in God with her love of a happy ending.

The Promise of Home

Kathryn Springer

Love Inspired

™ LOVE INSPIRED BOOKS

ISBN-13: 978-0-373-81624-8

THE PROMISE OF HOME

Copyright © 2012 by Kathryn Springer

www.LoveInspiredBooks.com

Printed in U.S.A.

The heavens declare the glory of God;
the skies proclaim the work of his hands.
Day after day they pour forth speech;
night after night they display knowledge.
There is no speech or language
where their voice is not heard.
Their voice goes out into all the earth,
their words to the ends of the world.
—*Psalms* 19:1–4

To my editor, Emily Rodmell,
for your attention to detail and commitment
to excellence (and also for smiley faces
in the margins during the revision process).
It is a blessing to work with you!

Chapter One

❧

"Please follow the highlighted route—"

Jenna Gardner tapped the tiny screen on the GPS and silenced the voice of her invisible navigator once and for all. Not only because the high-tech gadget seemed to be as confused as she was by the tangled skein of roads winding around Mirror Lake, but because Jenna was tempted to take its advice.

She wanted to follow the highlighted route right back to her condo in the Twin Cities.

"You passed it, Aunt Jenna!"

A panicked cry reminded her that going home wasn't an option. Not for awhile, anyway.

Jenna glanced in the rearview mirror. Once again, she experienced a jolt at the sight of the two children in the backseat.

Silver blond hair. Delicate features. Wide blue eyes. Jenna had met Logan and Tori for the first time only three days ago. The children were practically strangers.

Strangers who were the mirror image of her younger sister, Shelly, as a child.

For a split second, Tori met Jenna's gaze. Then she buried her face in the tattered scrap of pink flannel that doubled as a blanket.

Jenna pressed her lips together to prevent a sigh from escaping.

One step forward, two steps back, she reminded herself. The five-year-old girl was adjusting to the idea of having an aunt the same way Jenna was getting used to the idea of having a niece and nephew.

"You have to turn around," Logan insisted.

"Are you sure?" Jenna tipped her Ray-Bans down and tried to peer through the hedge of wild sumac that bordered the road. "I don't see anything."

"Uh-huh. It's back there." Logan, the self-appointed spokesman for the two siblings, nodded vigorously.

Under the circumstances, Jenna was willing to give the boy the benefit of the doubt. She put the car in reverse and began to inch backwards.

In Minneapolis, a dozen horns would have instantly chastised her for the move. But here in the north woods of Wisconsin, the only complaint Jenna heard came from a squirrel perched on a branch near the side of the road. More than likely voicing its opinion on her presence rather than her driving skills.

She spotted a wide dirt path that could have been—if a person possessed a vivid imagination—a driveway.

Pulling in a deep breath, Jenna gave the steering wheel a comforting pat as she turned off the road. Her back teeth rattled in time with the suspension as the vehicle bumped its way through the potholes.

Logan leaned forward and pointed to something up ahead. "There it is."

Well, that explained why Jenna had driven right past it.

She'd been looking for a *house*.

The weathered structure crouched in the shadow of a stately white pine looked more like a shed. Jenna's gaze shifted from the rusty skeleton of an old lawn mower to the faded sheets tacked up in the windows.

Oh, Shelly.

Why hadn't her younger sister admitted that she needed help? Why hadn't she accepted Jenna's offer to move in with her after Logan was born?

Throughout her pregnancy, Shelly had claimed that she and her musician boyfriend, Vance, planned to marry before the baby arrived. But when Jenna had visited her eighteen-year-old sister in the maternity wing of a Madison hospital, there hadn't been a ring on Shelly's finger. Not only that, she'd been alone. Faced with a choice, Vance had decided that a gig at a club in Dubuque was more important than being present for the birth of his child.

Shelly had made excuses for him—the same way their mother had made excuses for their father every time he'd walked out the door.

While Jenna was pleading with Shelly to return to Minneapolis with her, Vance had sauntered into the room. The guy might have been a mediocre guitar player, but his acting skills were nothing short of amazing. He'd apologized to Shelly for not being there and promised that she and the baby could travel with the band as their "good luck charms."

When Jenna had asked her sister if she was willing to sentence her child to the nomadic lifestyle they'd experienced while growing up, Vance had turned on her. Accused her of being a troublemaker. He'd convinced Shelly that Jenna was jealous of their relationship and didn't want them to be happy.

The stars in Shelly's eyes had blinded her to the truth. She had embraced Vance—and turned her back on her only sister.

Jenna hadn't seen or heard from her again. Had

no idea where Shelly was or even how she and Logan were doing.

Until last week.

She'd been sitting at her desk, sipping an iced vanilla latte and working on her next column for *Twin City Trends,* when she received a telephone call from a social worker named Grace Eversea.

It didn't matter how gently the young woman had tried to break the news, each piece of information had punctured a hole in Jenna's heart.

A house fire. Shelly in a rehab center for prescription drug abuse. Seven-year-old Logan and Tori, the niece Jenna hadn't even known existed, in temporary foster care.

As the children's closest relative, Jenna had been asked if she would be willing to help. She could think of a dozen reasons why she shouldn't get involved and only two—very small—reasons why she should.

Forty-eight hours later, after being granted a temporary leave of absence from the magazine, Jenna had packed her bags and driven to Mirror Lake, a small town where people knew each other's name and each other's business.

The kind of place she had deliberately avoided for the past ten years.

Her plan had been to take her niece and nephew back to Minnesota. But when Jenna met with

Grace Eversea, the social worker had explained it would be in Logan and Tori's best interest to remain in familiar surroundings for the time being.

Jenna could see the wisdom in Grace's suggestion—especially after learning that Tori and Logan had run away when they'd heard that she was on her way to Mirror Lake to meet them.

Jenna and the children had already spent several days at the Mirror Lake Lodge at the invitation of Abby and Quinn O'Halloran, the couple who owned the charming bed-and-breakfast, but she didn't want to impose on the newlyweds' hospitality any longer than necessary.

Until Shelly returned, Jenna decided that her only option was to move into the cabin where the family had been living before the fire. She'd been assured there had been only minimal damage to the interior and the local fire chief had pronounced the structure safe and sound.

But now, looking at the place her niece and nephew had called home, Jenna wasn't sure she agreed with either description.

"Are we getting out, Aunt Jenna?" Logan ventured.

Jenna realized she hadn't moved.

"Of course we are." Forcing a smile, she slid out of the driver's seat and went around to open Tori's door. "You're first, Button."

A corner of the blanket dropped, unveiling a pair of periwinkle eyes that stared back at her with guarded apprehension.

Jenna recognized the look of someone who no longer trusted easily, and her heart wrenched. Within the space of a few weeks the little girl had been separated from her mother and then from Kate Nichols, the foster care mother she'd become attached to, before being placed in Jenna's care.

"It's okay, Tori." Logan patted his sister's hand and the sweetness of the gesture pierced Jenna's soul.

How many times had she comforted Shelly when they were growing up? Protected her from danger—both imaginary and real?

Jenna mentally pushed the thought away. Her life was different now. *She* was different now.

She reached for the buckle on the booster seat but Tori shrank back.

"Don't wanna get out!"

Jenna hesitated, wondering if the little girl was remembering the night of the fire. Once again, the reality of what she'd agreed to flooded through her, eroding her confidence. She wasn't a child psychologist. She wasn't even the type of person that small children flocked to.

When it came right down to it, Jenna knew she

was everything that two traumatized children didn't need.

But right now, she was all they had.

"What's the matter, sweetheart?" Jenna summoned the bright, confident smile that had taken her from proofreader to *Twin City Trend's* most popular columnist.

Tori leaned over and whispered something in her brother's ear.

"She's afraid of wolves." To his credit, Logan didn't laugh.

Jenna bent down and looked her niece in the eye. "You don't have to worry about wolves, sweetheart. They stay away from people."

Tori's gaze fixed on something over Jenna's shoulder. "Even that one?"

That one?

Jenna whirled around and felt her knees buckle.

An enormous animal, its shaggy coat a mottled patchwork of grays and browns, was slinking down the shoreline.

Keep going, keep going.

Almost as if it had heard Jenna's silent plea, the creature paused for a moment and lifted its nose to the wind.

The wedge-shaped head swung in their direction.

Jenna's breath gathered in her lungs as the animal changed direction and started to lope toward them.

* * *

Devlin McGuire had just finished unloading the last of the gear from his SUV when he heard a muffled shriek near the lake.

Definitely human. Unmistakably feminine.

Mirror Lake, both the town and the small body of water it had been named after, didn't attract many tourists in the summer but Dev had noticed lights in the windows of the vacant cabin next door the last time he'd been home.

He had hoped his new neighbors would have moved on by the time he returned, but apparently they were sticking around a little longer. Soaking up some sun and enjoying the peace and quiet of the lake.

Something Dev would have appreciated himself right about now.

Shouldering his canvas backpack, he took a step toward the cabin. Less than ten yards away, a shower with hot water waited. And a porterhouse steak in the freezer...

Another shriek. This one sent a flock of crows swirling into the air like smoke from a black powder rifle—and carried a distinct edge of panic.

Dev decided the porterhouse could wait a few more minutes.

Making his way through the narrow strip of woods that separated the two cabins, he caught a glimpse of a vehicle parked in the driveway. As he stepped into the clearing for a better look, he stopped short at the sight that greeted him.

A young woman sat on the hood—*the hood*—of a sleek, charcoal gray Audi, peering down at something…

Oh, no.

At the base of the front left tire, Dev spotted a large animal stretched out on the ground.

Adrenaline surged through his veins and carried him forward. He sprinted across the yard, boots crunching over the patches of sun-scorched grass.

The woman's head jerked up.

A shimmering curtain of silver blond hair parted to reveal the kind of face that ordinarily graced the cover of celebrity magazines. Porcelain skin. High cheekbones. Big blue eyes that, if it were possible, seemed to get even bigger when he skidded up to the car.

"What happened?" Dev ground out.

"It…it just came out of nowhere—"

Tourists.

Dev wasted a precious second to scowl at the woman. "How fast were you going, anyway?"

"Fast? I wasn't…I didn't *hit* it. I was—" A low growl snipped off the rest of the sentence and the woman skittered backward.

Dev dropped to his knees and the shaggy head snapped around, fangs bared around the object locked between its jaws.

Relief mixed with the adrenaline as Dev came face-to-face with a pair of intelligent, albeit guilty, brown eyes.

"Violet, no. Drop it."

"Violet?" the woman squeaked.

"That's her name." Dev held out his hand and received a soggy shoe with a ridiculously high heel in return. He scrubbed a thumb over a tooth mark in the leather, winced when it didn't come out. "I'm sorry she scared you. Violet might be the size of a Volkswagen Bug, but she's harmless."

"It…it looks like a wolf."

Which explained why she'd taken refuge on the hood of her car. Sort of.

"Your average timber wolf doesn't wear a collar." Dev buried his hand in the thick ruff of fur around the dog's neck and jingled a pink, heart-shaped tag as proof.

"I thought she was going to attack me."

Dev arched a brow. "So you threw a shoe at her?"

"I didn't *throw* it. It…fell off." She was glaring at him now, not Violet.

Dev was getting the distinct impression that the blame had somehow shifted from the dog to its owner.

Violet bumped his arm, her pink tongue unfurling in a cheerful doggy grin, content to let him clean up the mess she'd made. Typical.

Dev buried a sigh and reached out his hand to help the woman down.

She didn't move.

It occurred to Dev that he probably looked a little...rough. A razor hadn't touched his face for over a week and his camo fatigues had been washed in a spring—

The breeze shifted and Dev saw the straight little nose twitch.

—And dried by the campfire.

Yup. Now she thinks you're a serial arsonist.

He scraped up some of the manners that had gotten a little rusty from lack of use.

"I'm Dev McGuire."

"Jenna—" Her lips compressed as if she regretted revealing that much information. "Just... Jenna."

Dev wondered what he could say to reassure her that neither he—nor his dog—were a threat.

"I live next door."

Eyes as blue as the forget-me-nots scattered along the shoreline fixed on a point beyond his shoulder, as if she were gauging the distance between the two places.

Now she moved. *Away* from him.

Dev's lips tipped in a rueful smile.

Apparently that wasn't it.

Chapter Two

Jenna stiffened.

Was he *laughing* at her?

When she'd seen the animal hurtling across the patch of lawn like a furry twister, Jenna automatically slammed the car door to protect the children inside.

Which left her on the *outside*.

Faced with a decision—one hastened by the knowledge that the size and weight of something didn't necessarily reduce its capacity for speed—Jenna had vaulted onto the hood, sacrificing a shoe in the process.

So maybe she'd reacted—okay, shrieked. Once. Or had it been twice? But not very loudly. And only because the beast had pounced on one of her favorite Kate Spades as if it were a juicy T-bone steak.

Jenna had been trying to figure out a way to get back inside the car when *he* showed up.

Her heart had almost stopped at the sight of the man in camouflage emerging from the woods that bordered the property.

Jenna sneaked another look at Dev McGuire and what she saw didn't exactly put her mind at ease.

The man looked as unkempt as the *wolf-dog-public nuisance* now sitting sedately at his feet.

A swatch of sable hair, carelessly combed by the warm breeze skipping off the lake, had fallen across his broad forehead. Underneath a heavy growth of stubble, the features were lean and defined, a pleasing clash of sharp angles and rugged planes. Tiny lines fanned out from eyes that should have been hazel or chocolate brown, not a pale amber that reminded Jenna of clover honey.

"I can replace the shoes if necessary." Dev McGuire broke the silence that had fallen between them and shot the dog a wry look. "It wouldn't be the first time I've had to make…ah, restitution for damages."

Jenna didn't doubt that for a minute.

"That's not necessary." She replaced her shoe and slid off the opposite side of the car.

Dev looked amused, as if he'd guessed that she wanted to keep her distance. Between him *and* his dog.

"If you ever do see a wolf, Just Jenna, I would recommend taking shelter *inside* the car."

"I'll keep that in mind," Jenna said stiffly. "I appreciate you coming over to get your dog, but don't let me keep you any longer—"

"Can we get out now?" A small voice piped up from inside the car.

Jenna had been waiting for Tori to talk to her all morning but these weren't exactly the words she'd wanted to hear.

She winced when her neighbor's focus shifted to the backseat, where two small faces were framed in the window, noses pressed against the glass.

Jenna hadn't forgotten about her niece and nephew, she just didn't want to draw attention to the fact they were there.

She pinned on a smile. "In a minute, sweetheart."

"When the wolf is gone?"

"It's not a wolf. It's just a...dog." A very large, ferocious-looking dog. Named after a small, delicate flower.

"Oh." A pause. "Can I pet it?"

Now that Dev McGuire had cleared up the mystery concerning what type of animal had scared her nearly to death, Jenna should have anticipated the request. One of the reasons Tori hadn't wanted to leave the bed-and-breakfast was because she'd gotten so attached to Mulligan and Lady, Abby and Quinn's dogs.

The O'Hallorans had encouraged Jenna to bring

the children back anytime to play with their pets, but the generous offer hadn't stemmed the flow of Tori's tears. To her niece, the dogs represented something else she'd been forced to leave behind.

"I don't think that's—" A good idea. *Safe*.

While Jenna silently sifted through her options until she found the most tactful response, Dev McGuire reached out and opened the car door.

The two kids that tumbled out of the backseat were miniature replicas of the woman who held Dev responsible for her recent wardrobe malfunction.

"Hi." Dev squatted down in front of the boy. Out of the corner of his eye, he saw Jenna advancing like a mama bear protecting her cubs. "I'm Dev. And you are—"

"Logan J. Gardner," came the serious response.

Dev held back a smile. "It's nice to meet you, Logan J. Gardner."

"And this is Tori." Logan gestured to the blonde pixie hiding behind him.

When Dev turned his attention to the little girl, she dipped her chin and studied the toes of her scuffed sneakers.

"It's nice to meet you, too, Tori."

She peeked at him through a fringe of golden lashes. "Your dog is pretty."

Violet tossed her head and preened as if she'd

understood, even though Dev was certain no one had ever used that particular word to describe her before.

"Do you like dogs?" he asked.

Tori nodded shyly.

"Well, she likes kids."

"For breakfast?" Dev heard Jenna say under her breath.

She stopped several feet away, hovering in the background like a Black Hawk helicopter, ready to swoop in and rescue her children at the first sign of danger.

Dev wondered what had happened to make her so suspicious.

Or maybe it was him she didn't trust. The last two weeks, Dev had spent more time in the woods than polite society. Not that he was complaining—most of the time he preferred it that way.

"Violet likes to have her ears scratched. Right here." Dev demonstrated and the dog growled her appreciation. Three pairs of eyes widened at the sound. "Don't worry. That's the noise she makes when she's happy."

"That's what she did when she picked up Aunt Jenna's shoe," Logan whispered.

Aunt Jenna.

The relief that arrowed through Dev didn't make any sense.

From the top of her shining hair to the tips of

her pedicure, Just Jenna was *not* his type. She was beautiful, no doubt about it, but everything about her shouted high maintenance. Stylish clothing. Simple but expensive jewelry.

Not to mention she was still looking at him the way she would a ketchup stain on her white jeans.

Jenna reminded him too much of Elaina Hammond. His ex-fiancé had always insisted on having the "best" of everything. The relationship ended when they'd no longer agreed on what that meant.

"Can I pet Violet, Aunt Jenna?" Tori repeated. "Please?"

Jenna tossed the dog a dubious glance. Fortunately, what Violet lacked in looks, she more than made up for in doggy smarts. She thumped her tail a few times and wiggled her eyebrows, a veritable canine poster child for good manners.

Jenna sighed. "I suppose so."

"Me, too." Logan dropped to his knees in front of the dog, whose lips peeled back to expose a row of gleaming white teeth.

Dev heard an audible gulp.

"Don't worry. She's smiling at you," he said. "Violet, meet Logan J. Gardner."

The boy tentatively reached out a hand and his mouth dropped open in amazement when Violet lifted a paw the size of a snowshoe for him to shake.

"See? She's very well trained," Dev murmured.

Jenna turned one slim ankle to examine her shoe and Dev almost laughed.

Point taken.

"What kind of dog is she?" Logan asked.

"According to the vet, mostly German shepherd and husky." Dev ruffled the dog's ears. "I found her running loose in the woods last summer when she was a pup. It took a few days and two packages of hotdogs to get her to trust me. That's how she got her name," he added. "She was shy as a violet."

Tori plopped down in the grass and Violet cemented their new friendship by swiping the girl's cheek with her tongue. Tori drew back, giggling.

"See Aunt Jenna! She doesn't bite."

"Only shoes." Dev tipped a smile at Jenna.

A smile she didn't return.

"I'm sure Mr. McGuire has things to do today. And so do we." Jenna glanced at the cabin and Dev was pretty sure he saw her...shudder?

Wait a second.

"You're *staying* here?" The moment Dev had laid eyes on Jenna, he'd dismissed the notion she'd been staying in the cabin and assumed she had somehow gotten lost and ended up mistaking the long driveway for a road. It happened all the time in an area where the locals had a tendency to give out directions based on natural landmarks rather than official signs.

"We have to." Logan sidled closer to his sister. "So our Mom knows where to find us."

Dev had no idea what that meant, but for a split second, he saw Jenna's composure slip. The flash of vulnerability an unexpected, almost startling, contrast to the confidence she wore with the same ease as her designer labels.

The speed in which Jenna had recovered from her initial embarrassment over their unusual introduction, restoring both her dignity and poise as swiftly as she'd replaced her shoe, told Dev she placed a high value on both.

But something also told Dev that Jenna was totally out of her element here. And not only because she looked like the type of woman whose idea of roughing it was a hotel where the guests were greeted by a valet, not an oversize mutt with a penchant for leather shoes.

Dev watched a chipmunk disappear through a crack in the foundation and imagined an entire colony of the furry little critters living under the porch. Not the kind of neighbors Just Jenna would choose if given a choice.

Then again, judging from the wary looks Dev had been receiving, she probably wouldn't have chosen him, either.

Keep your eyes open, Dev, Jason had liked to say. *God puts certain people in your path for a reason.*

After several years of soul searching, Dev no longer found those words difficult to believe. Even if he did spend long periods of time in the woods to reduce the risk of it happening.

But why would God deposit a reminder of the life he'd walked away from—even worse, a strikingly *pretty* reminder—less than a hundred yards from his front door?

There could only be one reason that Dev could think of.

He was being punished for something.

"There's a bed-and-breakfast about two miles from here," Dev said slowly. "I'm sure you'd be more comfortable there."

And, to be honest, so would he. One of the reasons Dev had turned his late grandfather's summer cabin into a permanent residence was because it provided the solitude he craved. If the owner of the cabin next door started renting it out on a regular basis, Dev would have to buy the place in order to prevent an influx of tourists from invading his privacy.

"We were just there," Tori piped up. "Abby has a dog named Mulligan, but he's not as big as Violet."

"We had to stay there because of the fire but Grace—she's our social worker—told us it was okay for us to come back home now," her brother added.

Dev's attempt to make sense of the conversation was sabotaged by a single word. His gaze swung to Jenna.

"What fire?"

Jenna debated what—if anything—to tell Devlin McGuire.

For a girl who transferred the details of her personal life to print for hundreds of devoted readers each week, she was curiously loathe to share any of them with *him*.

Unfortunately, the children didn't seem to share her reservations, forcing Jenna to question her initial impression of her niece and nephew. Maybe Logan and Tori weren't quiet. Maybe they were simply quiet around *her*.

She decided to give their neighbor the condensed version.

"No one was hurt and it didn't cause any major damage." At least, not to the cabin itself. Jenna still wasn't sure what lasting effects that night had had on her niece and nephew.

"And you were *here* at the time?" Dev persisted.

"Me and Logan were." Tori looked down at the ground. "And our mom."

"She's in the hospital," Logan said.

Dev's eyebrows dipped together in a frown and Jenna knew what he was thinking. "Not because of the fire," she said quickly. "She's there…for other reasons."

"Aunt Jenna's staying with us until Mom gets better." He looked at her for confirmation.

"That's right." Jenna masked her concern for Shelly, wishing she knew how long that would be.

She'd called the treatment center several days ago and asked to speak with her sister, only to be informed that Shelly wasn't accepting phone calls.

Jenna hadn't known where to turn for answers.

At Kate Nichols's suggestion, she had contacted Jake Sutton, the local chief of police who'd been at the scene the night of the fire. All he'd been able to discover was that Shelly had rented the cabin at the beginning of the summer and kept to herself.

Strange as it seemed, especially given a small town's propensity toward gossip, the police chief's assessment had proven to be correct. Kate had made some inquiries, too, and none of her regular customers at the Grapevine Cafe knew anything about Shelly.

Including, it seemed, her closest neighbor.

"I'm sorry about your mom."

The compassion Jenna heard in Dev's husky voice was a confusing contrast to the man's rough exterior.

But she didn't *need* confusing. Not right now.

"Mom's been sick a long time," Logan said, a shadow passing through his eyes.

Tori bobbed her head in agreement. "She sleeps a lot."

Jenna released a careful breath. It was the first time the children had said anything that hinted at Shelly's addiction.

A part of her hadn't wanted to believe it was true. The police hadn't found any drugs on the premises, so Shelly hadn't been taken into custody the night of the fire. But according to Grace Eversea, it had been the wake-up call Shelly needed to admit she had a problem and seek treatment.

"We're asking God to make her better," Logan said, his expression earnest. "He can do that, can't he, Aunt Jenna?"

"Yes. He can."

It was Dev McGuire who broke the sudden silence. Because even if Jenna had been certain of the answer, she was sure the word would have gotten stuck inside the lump forming in her throat.

For the children's sake, she hoped he was right.

"Is there anything I can do?" Dev was looking at her now, not the children. The genuine concern reflected in his eyes threatening to sever the fragile hold on her self-control.

"I'm fine." Jenna heard herself repeat the words that had served as an effective shield over the years.

And even though Dev nodded, she had the unsettling feeling that he could see right through it.

Watching him stride away, the dog loping along

at his side, Jenna was struck with a sudden, inexplicable urge to ask him to come back. But she'd learned long ago not to ask anyone for help. Not her neighbors. Not her teachers or classmates.

Not even God.

Chapter Three

"I'm afraid, Aunt Jenna."

Jenna felt a small hand slip into hers.

I am too, Jenna wanted to say. She was afraid of the role she'd taken on. Afraid she would somehow do the children more harm than good. But more than that, she was afraid of what would happen to Logan and Tori if Shelly didn't return within the next few days.

"It'll be all right." Jenna said, a reminder to herself as well as her niece. She gave Tori's hand a reassuring squeeze and worked the key into the rusty lock.

Stepping into the cabin was like stepping into the sauna at the fitness center. The air pressed in from all sides, making it difficult to breathe.

The first thing Jenna saw was the dark blister that marred the hardwood floor. According to the fire chief, Shelly had admitted that she'd fallen asleep on the couch with a cigarette in her hand. One of the embers had dropped between the cushions and started the cushions on fire.

Bile rose in Jenna's throat as the truth sank in.

She could have lost all three of them.

"I smell smoke." Logan stopped in the doorway, a worried look on his face.

"That's because the windows are shut, sweetheart." Crossing the room, Jenna stripped off the sheet tacked over the window and pushed it open. Immediately, a breeze from the lake began to filter into the room, caressing her face like a cool hand on a feverish brow.

"Better?"

Logan nodded and took a cautious step into the room.

Jenna had a feeling that erasing the acrid scent of smoke from the air would be easier than erasing the memories of the night the children had been removed from their home.

"I'm going to find Princess," Tori said in a small voice. "She's my favorite stuffed animal but I was afraid to ask the p'liceman if we could go back and get her. She might be hiding 'cause she got scared."

"Come on, Tori. I'll help you look." Logan stepped in and took his little sister by the hand. They disappeared through a doorway off the living room, giving Jenna a few moments to explore the rest of the cabin alone.

Her heart sank as she surveyed the bleak interior.

From what Jenna could see, Shelly had made no attempt to turn the place into a home. There were no pictures on the walls. No personal touches that told her anything about her sister's life.

Growing up, Shelly had been the outgoing one, unafraid of taking risks when it came to life—and love.

And look where it got her, Jenna thought.

The children's last name was still Gardner, which led her to believe that Vance and her sister had never married. Where was he? Had he eventually grown tired of the responsibility of a family and walked out, the same way Jenna's father had when she and Shelly were children?

She and Shelly had both felt the sting of his rejection. But while her younger sister had dreamed of finding someone to take care of her, Jenna had learned to take care of herself.

She'd never imagined those lessons would launch a popular magazine column, but that's exactly what had happened. Jenna didn't love the attention as much as she loved encouraging other women to become successful and independent.

Something she hadn't been able to do for her own sister.

Jenna picked a towel off the floor and walked into the tiny kitchen. Unopened letters littered the table and the sink was filled with dirty dishes.

She turned on the faucet and the pipes rattled before spitting out a stream of rusty water.

Jenna closed her eyes.

What had she been thinking?

They were leaving. Now. Familiar surroundings or not. There had to be something to rent in Mirror Lake while they waited for Shelly to return.

This place...the aura of neglect and poverty. It reminded her of things she had spent years trying to forget.

Jenna followed the sound of voices to a bedroom only slightly larger than the walk-in closet in her apartment. The knotty pine walls appeared to be in fairly good condition, but a network of tiny cracks branched out from a central fault line in the plaster ceiling. Swags of cobwebs hung from the light fixture above her head.

Tori sat cross-legged on the frayed carpet, rummaging through a cache of toys stashed in a plastic bin at the foot of one of the bunk beds, while Logan was already unpacking the contents of his backpack.

Both the children looked up and smiled as Jenna entered the room.

Tori cuddled a stuffed dog in her lap. "This is Princess, but I think she looks like Violet, don't you?"

Jenna didn't want to think about Violet. Thinking about Violet made her think of Violet's *owner*.

Her cheeks grew warm as she remembered the glint of amusement in Devlin McGuire's eyes when he'd suggested that she take refuge inside of her car if she ever crossed paths with a real wolf.

Once they found another place to live, the chances of seeing her neighbor again would be slim. As humiliating as their first meeting had been, Jenna was no hurry for there to be another.

She moved to sit on the edge of the bed and her ankle connected with a solid object underneath the frame.

"Ouch." Wincing, Jenna reached down and pulled out an unopened can of paint.

"That's ours." Tori flashed a shy smile. "Mom promised she would paint our room."

"When she felt better," Logan added.

Jenna glanced at the receipt from the hardware store taped to the lid. The paint had been purchased over a month ago. Shelly hadn't been able to find the time—or the energy—to tackle a project that, given the size of the bedroom, wouldn't have taken more than a few hours to complete.

How many other promises had her sister broken

along the way? And at what age would Logan and Tori stop believing them?

"We can paint it and surprise Mommy, can't we, Aunt Jenna?" Tori's voice tugged her back to the present. "It's pink. Me an' Logan's favorite color."

"It's *your* favorite color," her brother muttered.

"You said you liked it!" Tori thrust out her chin, daring him to disagree.

"No, I didn't." The tips of Logan's ears turned red. "I said it was okay if *you* liked it."

Jenna recognized the small sacrifice her nephew had made to keep Tori happy, and something stirred in her heart.

It looked like she was going to have to make one, too.

Because like it or not, for now, the children had told Dev McGuire the truth.

This was home.

With a flick of his wrist, Dev released the line on his fishing pole. Sunlight sparked off the lure right before it sliced through the gleaming surface of the water and disappeared. He turned the handle on the reel and immediately felt a tug of resistance.

"I think we've got one," he told Violet.

The dog barked her encouragement, tail waving like a victory banner as Dev set the hook and brought in a bluegill the size of his hand. Not bad for the first cast of the day.

As he removed the hook from the fish's mouth, a furtive movement in the reeds caught his eye. Violet noticed it, too, and immediately set off to investigate.

"If it's black with a white stripe, leave it alone," Dev called after her. "Remember what happened last summer. You lost in the first round."

And Dev hadn't been able to so much as *look* at a glass of tomato juice since.

Violet ignored him and plunged headfirst into the cattails.

"Hey!"

Her quarry—a barefoot, towheaded boy— scrambled out the other side.

Logan J. Gardner.

So. Just Jenna had actually stuck it out for a night. If Dev were a gambling man, he would have bet she'd packed her Gucci bag and headed to a five-star hotel before a person could say *complimentary facial.*

Violet barked at the pint-sized trespasser, who stood rooted in place, shoulders hunched, his cheeks red with embarrassment at having been caught spying on the neighbors.

"Don't pay any attention to Violet." Dev cast out his line again, acting as if there were nothing at all unusual about discovering a boy lurking in the reeds at seven o'clock in the morning. "Hide-and-seek happens to be number two on her list of favorite games."

The tension in Logan's shoulders eased a little. He reached out and gave the dog's nose a tentative pat. It was all the encouragement Violet needed. She retrieved a piece of birch wood floating in the shallow water and dropped it at the boy's feet.

Dev shook his head. "Fetching sticks is number one."

With a sideways look at Dev, Logan dutifully picked up the stick and threw it. Violet sprang forward, massive paws churning ruts in the sand as she chased it down the shoreline.

Logan shuffled closer, pushing his hands into the pockets of his cargo shorts. "Did you catch anything yet?"

"Just getting started." Dev tried another spot further from the lily pads. "Do you like to fish?"

The thin shoulders rolled in a shrug. "My friend Jeremy does. He said he'd teach me this summer, but I don't know if I'd be any good at it."

But he wanted to try. Dev could see it in Logan's eyes.

"There's one way to find out." He held out the fishing pole.

Logan eased a look over his shoulder.

A look Dev instantly recognized. He'd been that age once upon a time.

"Does your aunt know you're over here?"

Logan suddenly became absorbed in watching an emerald green dragonfly fanning its wings near his feet. "She said I could go outside."

Dev took that as a no. He should have known Jenna wouldn't approve of her nephew venturing down to the lake alone. Or crossing the property line.

But apparently Jenna didn't know that one had to be specific when it came to small boys.

A memory somehow managed to slip through a tiny crack in the wall surrounding Dev's grief.

When he wasn't much older than Logan, Dev's father had given him and Jason some leftover wood from one of the construction sites. He hadn't told them *not* to use it to build a ramp. And he hadn't told them *not* to ride their bicycles off the end of said ramp.

Dev had tried to point that out on the way to the emergency room while Jason sat in the backseat, cradling a broken arm. Unfortunately, his father hadn't appreciated his logic.

You're the oldest, Devlin. I expect more from you.

Those words had become a familiar refrain while Dev was growing up, playing in the background while he was being groomed to take over the family construction business. Dev didn't mind. He'd embraced the challenges—and the advantages—that came with being the oldest son of Brent McGuire.

In college, Jason had chosen a different path. One that had had Dev shaking his head in confusion at the time. If only he'd had the opportunity to tell his brother that he finally understood.

"You've got another one!" Logan's excited cry jerked Dev from the past with the same urgency as the fish tugging on the end of his line.

Dev set the hook and turned to Logan. "Do you want to bring it in?"

"Sure," the boy said eagerly, his previous hesitation forgotten as he reached for the pole.

"Reel it in nice and slow…" Dev instructed as he bent down to retrieve the net.

Logan shot him a panicked look. "You should take it now. It's going to get away."

"No, it won't. You're doing great."

"Look how big it is!" Logan's eyes grew wide as Dev knelt down on the dock and scooped up the fish.

"Here you go." Dev carefully removed the hook from the bluegill's mouth and dropped it into a bucket of water. "It's definitely a keeper. I'll put it on the stringer so you can take it home."

"Really?"

"You catch it, you keep it."

Eyes shining, Logan squatted down to admire the fish. "Maybe we can have it for lunch."

"Maybe." A smile lifted the corners of Dev's lips. If only he could see Jenna's face when she saw the catch of the day.

"Logan?"

Dev glanced over his shoulder at the sound of a familiar voice behind them.

It looked as though his wish was about to come true.

Jenna's heart skipped a scheduled beat when Dev McGuire turned around. At some point in the last twelve hours, a startling transformation had occurred.

The heavy growth of stubble that had shadowed the angular jaw was gone, enhancing the clean lines of Dev's chiseled features. The bright morning sunlight coaxed out hints of bronze in the sable hair that Jenna hadn't noticed before.

In faded jeans and a dark green T-shirt that accentuated broad shoulders and muscular arms, Dev looked like a man totally at ease in his surroundings.

And way too attractive for her peace of mind.

Jenna stopped, suddenly reluctant to venture any closer.

"Look at the fish I caught, Aunt Jenna!" Logan shouted, jumping up and down on the dock like a pogo stick and pointing to a metal bucket near his feet.

"I wanna see it, too!" Tori broke free from Jenna's hold and scampered toward her brother.

It was a conspiracy, no doubt about it.

Jenna picked her way down to the shoreline, the heels of her shoes sinking into the spongy ground with every step.

"Hurry up, Aunt Jenna!"

Aware that Dev was watching her approach, Jenna grabbed the wooden post on the end of the dock. The narrow platform jutting over the water hadn't looked quite so precarious from a distance. As Jenna gingerly stepped onto the first section, Violet decided to join her.

The dog, marinated in lake water and coated with a fine layer of sand, lowered its shaggy head and barked at her.

Nice to see you again? Get off my property?

Jenna had no idea what Violet was attempting to communicate, but she was hesitant to take another step until she knew for sure.

"Violet, no." Dev strode toward them. "Look out, Jenna. She's going to—"

Shake.

That must have been the word Dev had been looking for.

If only he would have said it *faster*.

Chapter Four

Jenna jumped backward to avoid the shower. The heel of her shoe found a weak spot in the weathered boards and opened a space for her entire foot to go through.

She attempted to wiggle free before Dev noticed her dilemma.

"Do you need some help?"

Jenna tried not to groan.

He'd noticed her dilemma.

"I'm—"

"Fine," Dev interrupted. "I think you made that clear yesterday. But at the moment it looks like you're...stuck."

Unfortunately, Jenna couldn't argue with the assessment. She *was* stuck. Stuck in the kind of town she'd spent the majority of her life wanting to leave. Stuck in a cabin that let more mosquitoes in than it kept out, instead of her condo with its enclosed balcony and manicured lawn.

No dogs allowed.

But worst of all, it appeared as though Jenna was stuck with a neighbor who'd seen her in what could only be described as less than ideal—okay, *humiliating*—situations.

Twice.

"Don't move—" Dev began.

Jenna moved. And winced when a jagged splinter thwarted her attempt to shake her foot free from the shoe.

Shaking his head, Dev knelt down and ignored her strangled protest.

Jenna tried to lean as far away from him as she could. But considering her foot was wedged between two boards, it wasn't nearly far enough.

A large hand curved around her ankle. The unexpected touch caught Jenna off guard. And sent an equally unexpected jolt of electricity running through her.

"Hold still," Dev commanded. "You're as jumpy as a tree frog."

A tree frog. Now there was something a girl dreamed of being compared to.

"What's taking so long?" Jenna found her view blocked by a broad shoulder.

"I'm trying to decide which one to save. Your

shoe or your foot." Dev slanted a look at her, the amusement in his eyes a contrast to his solemn tone.

"That's not funny." But even as she said the words, Jenna felt a bubble of laughter rising in her chest.

What would her readers think if they saw City Girl, their favorite columnist, now? Jenna was relieved this particular moment in her life would never make it into print!

"You should think about investing in something a little more—" A gentle tug. "—practical."

Jenna wanted to argue that this pair of shoes had been the source of inspiration for the most popular column she'd ever written.

"In the Right Pair of Shoes, A Girl Can Go Anywhere."

"I mean, considering they're practically stilts, I can see you get decent clearance," Dev went on. "But they can't possibly be comfortable."

"They happen to be exactly right for where I live." Jenna ignored the part about them being comfortable. "Concrete sidewalks. Foliage growing in pots. Parks with leash laws…" Her attempt to deny the humor in the situation was too much. She grinned down at him.

And Dev released her so abruptly that she almost lost her balance again. The laughter faded from his eyes.

"That might be true, but these things won't

last a week and neither—" He stopped, but Jenna knew what he'd been about to say.

Neither will you.

With as much dignity as she could muster, Jenna swished right past him on her impractical shoes.

If she wasn't determined to do everything in her power to be back in Minneapolis as soon as possible, it would have been oh so tempting to prove the man wrong.

Dev watched his neighbor sashay down the dock and felt like a first-class jerk.

Sorry, God, but you know I don't deal well with surprises.

Like finding out that Just Jenna had a sense of humor. Or the zap of attraction he'd felt when she cast that mischievous grin in his direction.

Dev hadn't felt that tongue-tied since a black bear had wandered into his campsite one night and lay down on the end of his sleeping bag. While he was inside of it.

A cold nose nudged his hand and Dev looked down. Violet's bushy eyebrows wiggled an apology.

"Only because I have to," Dev said in a low voice. After all, it was his own fault for owning a dog the size of a skid steer. "But sit here—and try to stay out of trouble."

Violet flopped onto her belly. Of course. *Now*

she listened to him. Leaving the dog in an expanding pool of lake water, he went to join the group assembled at the end of the dock.

"Dev let me reel it in all by myself," Logan was saying. The look of pride on the boy's face made Dev smile.

"Mr. McGuire," Jenna corrected her nephew.

"I don't mind if they call me Dev. 'Mr. McGuire' is too formal for fishing buddies." Not only that, every time Dev heard it he'd have to fight the urge to glance over his shoulder to make sure his father hadn't materialized behind him.

Brent McGuire would have viewed a few hours of early morning fishing as a complete waste of time.

In fact, his father believed that until Dev returned to take over the helm of the family business, his entire life was being wasted. Telephone conversations had become thinly disguised lectures on duty and responsibility. His mother kept a running list of everything Dev was "missing." It was the reason their relationship had been condensed to brief phone calls, spaced out over major holidays.

Dev didn't regret moving to Mirror Lake. No one here cared about the gold plaque on his door or his family pedigree. The locals respected his desire for privacy and left him alone. Dev had decided it was only fair to return the favor.

His life might not be the way Dev pictured it, what he'd lost couldn't be compared to everything he'd gained. The solitude, which in the beginning had seemed like a punishment, Dev had begun to view as a gift from God.

That's why he couldn't figure out why God had deposited a woman and two children practically outside his door. Especially a woman like Jenna, who looked as if she was dressed for a photo shoot and obviously preferred to see her fish breaded and served next to a side of coleslaw rather than swimming around in a bucket.

"It smells funny." Tori, who'd pushed closer for a better view of the fish, wrinkled her nose.

For a split second, Jenna looked as if she were tempted to do the same.

Logan dismissed his little sister's comment and looked at his aunt with a hopeful expression, waiting for her opinion.

"It's very slimy—" Jenna caught herself. "*Shiny.* Very shiny."

Logan beamed. "It's a keeper, right, Dev?"

"That's right." Was it his imagination, or was Jenna looking a little, er, green around the gills?

"And I get to take it home."

Forget-me-not blue eyes widened at Logan's announcement.

No, definitely not his imagination.

"B-but—"

"It's one of the rules of fishing." Dev interrupted Jenna midsputter.

"Rules?" She gazed at him with open skepticism.

"Unwritten, of course."

"Of course."

"You catch it, you keep it," Logan sang out.

"Exactly." Dev checked a smile.

"That's very…thoughtful…of you," Jenna said in a tone that hinted it was just the opposite.

"Can you take a picture of it, Aunt Jenna?" Logan asked. "I want to show Mom."

A shadow passed through Jenna's eyes but she nodded. "Of course, but I think you should be holding the fish so she can see how big it is."

"Can I hold it, too?" Tori wanted to know.

"I have an idea. Why don't I take the picture and all three of you can pose with the fish?" Dev couldn't resist.

"Okay!"

Jenna didn't join the chorus. She sighed and pulled a slim black gadget out of her pocket, the kind that did everything but clean your house.

Dev held out his hand and she reluctantly dropped the expensive little piece of technology into his calloused palm. Dev stood patiently through the brief tutorial that followed.

"Now, how should we set this up?" Jenna squinted at the sun. "Maybe—"

"I think I can take it from here." Dev lined up the shot. "Ready?"

Only two blond heads bobbed. In this instance, Dev went with the majority.

"Stand right there—Logan don't drop the fish." He took a step back and the trio came into focus. Logan with his proud, gap-toothed grin. Tori cheek to cheek with Violet, who'd managed to sneak into the frame. And Jenna, beautiful but somber.

Dev wondered what she was thinking.

She's thinking that you're going to drop her phone into the lake and cut off her only tie to civilization, an inner voice chided. *Take the picture.*

He snapped a few quick shots. "Okay, time to put the fish on a stringer so you can take him home with you."

"His name is Fred," Tori announced.

Everyone turned to stare at her.

"We're not going to name it." Logan rolled his eyes. "We're going to eat it."

Tori looked horrified by the thought. "We can't eat Fred."

"Toriiii." His sister's name rolled out on a groan. "That's what you're *supposed* to do."

"But his family will miss him," she wailed.

Logan sent a silent appeal to Dev for help.

"Sorry, bud. Your fish, your call." No way was

he going to weigh in on that decision. And one look at Jenna's face revealed whose side she was on.

Logan heaved a sigh. "Okay. But just this once."

"Just this once," Tori agreed cheerfully.

No one believed her.

"Come on." Dev grabbed the bucket and strode down the dock.

At the edge of the shoreline everyone, including Jenna, release a collective breath as Fred propelled himself into the deeper water with a graceful swish of his back tail fin. Along with the bluegill Dev had planned to have for supper that night.

Tori clapped her hands. "Fred's going home."

"I'm going to follow him." Logan leaped to his feet.

"Wait for me." Tori followed, chasing after her brother through the waves that lapped the shoreline. Violet tore after them, barking her approval.

Dev had a hunch his company was going to seem pretty boring from now on.

"They're good kids." Dev watched Logan pause to grab his little sister's hand when she stumbled in the wet sand.

"They are." There it was again. That brief flash of vulnerability Dev had seen in Jenna's eyes the day before. "Sometimes I'm not sure I'll be able to keep up with them."

"Another reason to wear something more practical on your feet." Dev couldn't resist teasing her a little. Call him a glutton for punishment, but he wanted to see that mischievous smile again.

"I do have another pair of shoes." Jenna's chuff of indignation stirred a ribbon of silver-blond hair on her forehead. "I just didn't think I'd *need* them. I didn't plan to be in Mirror Lake for more than a day or two."

Dev could relate. He'd arrived at his grandfather's old fishing cabin for a weekend. Five years ago.

"So what made you decide to stay?"

Jenna was silent for so long, Dev didn't think she was going to answer the question.

"My sister."

It was a little unsettling to discover they had something in common. Jenna had come to Mirror Lake because of her sister and Dev was there because of his brother.

"This is a good place." Dev watched a young bald eagle spin a lazy circle over the treetops. "Kids need room to roam."

Jenna's lips compressed, a sign she didn't agree with him. "That reminds me. I'm sorry that Logan interrupted your day. I guess I need to have a talk with him about boundaries."

Dev remembered the look of wonder on Logan's face when he'd offered him the fishing pole.

"I didn't mind. And he can fish off my dock anytime he wants to—"

Jenna was already shaking her head. "I don't think that's a good idea."

"It's safe as long as he's not down here alone. Even at the end of the dock, the water isn't over his head."

"That's not it. I don't want Logan or Tori to get too attached to…this place."

"I thought Logan said they lived here." From what the children had said the day before, he assumed their mother had bought it.

Jenna shook her head. "My sister rented the cabin for the summer. It's temporary. When she gets home, I'm hoping I can convince her to move closer to me."

From the expression on Jenna's face, that day couldn't come soon enough.

Why that bothered him, Dev didn't know. Especially since he'd dropped a not-so-subtle hint that she wouldn't last a week.

Tori skipped up to them and tugged on Jenna's arm. "I found a spider on a tree over there, Aunt Jenna. Do you want to take its picture, too?"

Too?

Dev glanced at Jenna and saw twin patches of color underline the sculpted cheekbones.

"No thanks, sweetie."

Logan joined them. "But it's bigger than the one you found this morning."

Dev had to ask. He just had to. "Did she scream?"

Logan thought about that. "A little."

"It was in the bathtub," Tori added. "And it was huuuge."

"Aunt Jenna took its picture. She said it was so big that we could put a leash on it and take it for a walk around the block—"

"Why don't you two go inside and get washed up?" Jenna cut in. "We haven't had breakfast yet."

As far as diversions went, it might not have been subtle but it was effective. The children headed toward the cabin. Dev grabbed hold of Violet's collar before she included herself in the invitation.

"So. A spider." Dev's lips twitched.

"I'm sure you've seen them before," Jenna said tartly.

"Not one that I could put a leash on and take for a walk around the block."

Jenna whipped out her phone again and scrolled through the pictures, stopping at the close-up of a spider roughly the size of the designer dog Elaina had carried around in her purse.

Dev blinked. Okay, it *was* that big.

"What did you do? Throw your shoe at it?" He'd been kidding...until he saw the guilty look on Jenna's face.

"You threw your shoe at it?"

"Yes, but I didn't think I'd actually *hit* it."

"I'm shocked."

"So was I." The husky laugh that followed packed more of a punch than Jenna's smile.

While Dev was recovering from the impact, she veered toward the cabin. Tossed a smug look over her shoulder.

"And *you* said they weren't practical."

Dev closed his eyes, but there she was—engraved in his memory—ready to return at a moment's notice.

So maybe Jenna wasn't a clone of Elaina, but she was obviously a city girl.

There was no point getting involved with someone who'd made no secret of the fact that she couldn't wait to leave Mirror Lake, the only place in the world that Dev wanted to be.

Jenna was right. Boundaries weren't such a bad idea.

For all of them.

Chapter Five

"Helloooo!"

A lilting voice rose above the rattle of the ancient ceiling fan that paddled in lazy circles above Jenna's head, dispersing humid air to every corner of the cabin.

The children, who'd been playing a lively game of Go Fish while Jenna washed the breakfast dishes, leaped to their feet.

"It's Kate!" Logan shouted on his way to the door.

Jenna tried not to feel envious. Even though the cafe owner had gone out of her way to make Jenna feel welcome since she'd arrived in Mirror Lake, the children's exuberant greeting was a painful reminder that Kate Nichols knew her niece and nephew better than she did.

The petite redhead scooped up Tori and anchored her against one slender hip. "How are you doing, strawberry shortcake?"

Tori giggled. "I'm not shortcake."

"That's right." Kate's clover green eyes twinkled. "You're much sweeter." She planted a kiss on the little girl's temple and reached down to ruffle Logan's bangs. "How are you doing, buddy?"

"I caught a fish this morning."

"Well, that answers that question." Kate winked at Jenna over his head.

"It's good to see you, Kate," Jenna said. Although she'd hoped to have the cabin looking a bit more presentable before anyone stopped over.

She'd planned to do some cleaning and then take the children into town to pick up some groceries. A quick inventory of the cupboards had yielded a few cans of soup and a box of macaroni and cheese. Fortunately, Abby had insisted Jenna take a basket of homemade cinnamon rolls and a quiche with her when they'd left the lodge, so breakfast had been covered.

"I'm sorry I didn't call first." Kate set Tori down on the floor. "We wanted to surprise you."

We?

As if on cue, a young woman with a cap of cherry-cola curls trudged into the cabin, a colorful plastic tote gripped in each hand.

"'Morning, Jenna!"

Jenna recognized the visitor immediately. Zoey Decker and her fiancé, Matthew Wilde, were close friends of the O'Hallorans and had dropped by the inn to visit while Jenna and the children were staying there.

The couple planned to exchange their vows at the inn on Christmas Eve, and Abby was in charge of the event.

"Zoey." Jenna greeted her cautiously.

"I hope we're not too early," Zoey sang out, and in the next breath, "Where do you want this stuff?" The question was directed at Kate, who pointed to the kitchen.

Jenna's gaze cut back to the woman clearly in charge of the operation. "What's going on?"

"A housewarming party," Kate said.

"You provide the house, we provide the party." Zoey swept past her with a grin.

Kate saw Jenna's confusion and took pity on her. "We're here to help you spruce things up a bit. Stanley Lambert, the guy who owns this cabin, is one of my regulars at the cafe and he let it sit empty for years. I figured if he hasn't updated his wardrobe for forty years, chances are he hasn't done anything to this place, either."

While Jenna was recovering from the shock of the unexpected invasion, the screen door swung open again. Warm, blue-gray eyes peered at Jenna over an enormous picnic basket. The fingers of one hand fanned a greeting.

"Emma Sutton." Kate took charge of the introductions this time. "This is Jenna Gardner—

Logan and Tori's aunt." She smiled at Jenna. "You already met Emma's husband, Jake."

"Hi." Emma flashed a friendly smile.

Sutton. The police chief. Jenna searched the woman's face but didn't see a hint of judgment that she'd met Jake under less than ideal circumstances. He was the one who'd called Grace Eversea the night that Shelly had started the fire.

"It's nice to meet you," she murmured.

Emma set the picnic basket down on the scarred Formica table. "Logan and my son, Jeremy, have gotten to be good friends over the past few weeks."

Logan's face lit up when he heard the boy's name. "Is Jeremy here?"

"Are you kidding? There was no way he was going to stay home once he found out where I was going. He's unloading some things from the car."

"Cool! I'm going outside, Aunt Jenna." Logan dashed out the door, Tori at his heels.

"Jeremy is twelve and very responsible," Emma assured her. "He doesn't mind keeping an eye on Logan and Tori while we work."

Kate frowned. "Speaking of work…where's Abby?"

"I'm right here." Abby O'Halloran breezed into the cabin, dropped a box into the lap of the lumpy tweed recliner and reeled Jenna in for a hug.

A *hug.* As if they'd known each other forever

rather than just a few days. Then she stepped back and looked Jenna straight in the eye.

"How are you?"

Jenna opened her mouth, ready to give her standard response, but something in Abby's compassionate gaze seemed to require an honest response.

"I'm...not sure."

Abby nodded, as if that made perfect sense. "That's why we're here."

Zoey parked her hands on her hips. "Where should we start?"

Jenna felt her control slipping. "Really...you don't have to—"

"Of course we don't." Kate cut off her protest, her brisk tone matching her movements as she began to unpack an arsenal of cleaning supplies. "We *want* to. You move to a small town, you get the small town treatment."

Jenna had already experienced that, and the memories weren't pleasant ones. People had either ignored her family or gossiped about them, but no one had ever offered to help.

"Jake mentioned the fire didn't do much damage, but we figured a few little touches might make you feel more at..." Emma's voice trailed off.

For the first time, the visitors seemed to become aware of their surroundings. The dark paneling that shadowed the walls. The shabby furnishings.

The scorch mark on the scuffed hardwood floor, evidence of what could have been a fatal mistake.

Forget the fact that she lived in a gated community with a waiting list that stretched into the next decade. Jenna was suddenly eight years old again, facing the girls that had drifted over to meet her the day she'd moved into the neighborhood.

She had invited them in to play, but the pigtail posse created their own game. They'd spent the morning poking fun at the tiny garage apartment. And at her.

The scenario continued through high school. Different towns, the same response. Being measured by her peers and found wanting. Old insecurities, the ones Jenna thought she had put behind her, began to creep in as Kate and her friends surveyed the cabin.

"It's got a lot of potential," Abby declared.

Emma saw Jenna's expression and laughed. "Abby's bed-and-breakfast needed three times this much work when she bought it. She welcomes a challenge."

"Which explains Quinn," Kate whispered.

Abby gave her friend a playful swat on the arm. "This from the woman who fell in love with my bossy big brother. Most people run in the opposite direction when they see Alex coming."

Zoey must have noticed Jenna's bemusement.

"They can be a little overwhelming, can't they?"

she said in a low voice. "The first time I met them, they bullied me into joining their knitting group."

Abby heard her. "Bullied isn't quite the word... oh, maybe it is. But you'll get used to us," she added with a bright smile at Jenna.

Jenna didn't contradict her, even though she knew she wouldn't be in Mirror Lake long enough to join a knitting group. Or any other kind of group, for that matter.

Watching the way the four friends interacted, with genuine affection and acceptance, Jenna wondered what it would be like to be included in their close-knit circle.

Other than a weekly cappuccino date with Caitlin Walsh, the image consultant Jenna had met while working on a special makeover issue for the magazine, the majority of Jenna's time and energy were devoted to her readers.

The door opened and an adolescent boy walked in, balancing a bulky object on his shoulder. Judging from the smoke blue eyes and sandy brown hair, this was Emma's son, Jeremy. He flashed a shy smile at Jenna before turning to Abby. "Where did you want this, Mrs. O'Halloran?"

Abby pointed to the floor. "Right over there."

Jenna watched Zoey and Kate kneel down and unroll the hand-hooked wool rug. A butter-yellow border outlined a stunning bouquet of wildflowers in the pattern. The colors brightened the room—

and completely covered the blackened area on the hardwood floor.

"This was delivered to the inn yesterday, but the order was wrong," Abby explained. "It was too small for the library...but I think it might be just right for you."

Tears stung the back of Jenna's eyes and she blinked them away before anyone noticed.

"It's perfect, Abby," Emma said. "And the colors just *happen* to coordinate with the curtains I brought over."

For some reason, the rest of the women smiled when she emphasized the word.

"How much do I owe you?" Jenna had read the home style section of *Twin City Trends* often enough to know that a custom designed rug this size would have cost a small fortune.

"It's a gift." Abby linked her arm through Jenna's. "A reminder that God provides exactly what we need when we need it."

Jenna didn't know how to respond to that. It was something she'd often heard Caitlin Walsh say, but she'd never experienced it before. It was risky to wait. To hope that someone would notice her. That someone would...care.

"He does," Abby murmured.

Jenna stared at her, afraid she'd voiced the thought out loud, but the other woman was already gliding away.

"We'll have this place looking like home in no time," Zoey said, a determined gleam in her eyes as she advanced on the dusty bearskin rug tacked to the wall.

"Okay, sisters." Kate tightened the knot on the bandana covering her copper curls as if she were preparing for battle. "Divide and conquer."

Dev tossed a piece of birch bark into the campfire and sat back to enjoy the shower of sparks as the flames consumed it. There had been a time when he would have scoffed at such simple entertainment. When he'd believed that a man who had time to sit by a campfire had too much time.

He took out his pocketknife and began to sharpen the end of a stick.

Violet, stretched out on a old trapper's blanket beside him, lifted her head and stared into the deepening shadows at the edge of the woods.

Dev had a hunch he knew what—or who—had caught the dog's attention.

For the past few days, Logan Gardner had been sneaking across the property line to play with Violet. And when he didn't show up, Violet had been sneaking across the property line to play with *him*.

Dev figured it was only a matter of time until Jenna marched over to register a formal complaint.

"Violet." He crooked a finger at the blanket,

earning a reproachful look. The same one he'd seen the last time he'd given her a bath. *"Stay."*

She flopped back down, her heavy sigh questioning the fairness of the command.

"Trust me—it's for your own good," Dev told the dog.

His, too. The less contact he had with Jenna the better. Dev had spent the last five years trying to simplify his life, and everything about the woman shouted complicated.

The fact that he hadn't been able to stop thinking about her proved it.

"Hi, Mr. McGuire." Logan slunk out of the woods a few seconds later, shoulders hunched as if he were unsure of his welcome. A coonskin cap, the kind sold at every souvenir store in the county, drooped over one bright blue eye.

"It's Dev, remember?"

Logan shuffled closer, the faux raccoon tail swinging over one shoulder like a furry pendulum. "I smelled smoke, and I wanted to make sure you and Violet were okay."

The anxious look in the boy's eyes reminded Dev that he'd recently witnessed a fire, one that hadn't been contained in a circle of stones. Jenna had claimed that no one had been hurt, but Dev knew from experience that not all injuries were visible on the outside.

Guilt tweaked his conscience. He'd been traveling a lot since the beginning of summer, but how could he have been ignorant of the fact there were two children living next door?

Other than the day he'd met Jenna, he hadn't heard a peep out of them. Not even Violet had alerted Dev to their presence.

"I appreciate your concern," he told Logan gently. "But it's just a campfire. I usually cook my dinner out here in the evenings."

Violet lifted her nose to sniff the raccoon tail and Logan giggled. "She thinks it's real."

"That's a great hat."

"Kate found it when she was cleaning the closet." Logan swept the cap off his head. Imitation fur sifted to the ground like needles on a dead spruce when he offered it to Dev to admire.

"Kate Nichols?" It was the only Kate that Dev knew. From what he'd heard, the perky cafe owner was the poster girl for hometown pride, scouting out unsuspecting victims to serve on the various committees she organized. Because of that, Dev gave the woman a wide berth on his occasional trips into town.

"She was our foster mom. Me an' Tori lived with her until Miss Eversea called Aunt Jenna." The matter-of-fact statement told Dev that foster parents and social workers weren't uncommon in Logan's world.

But where did Jenna fit? That's what he didn't know.

And if she has her way, you won't get the chance to find out, he reminded himself.

Dev handed the cap back to Logan. "Don't let Violet get hold of it," he warned. "I'm still missing a leather glove and one sheepskin slipper."

Logan plunked it back on his head. "Aunt Jenna wanted to throw it away."

"No way." Dev pretended to be shocked.

"She said it wasn't sanitary, but Kate told her that every explorer should have a hat like this."

"I agree." Dev matched his tone to the solemn look on Logan's face.

Violet rolled to her feet, bumping up against the boy in a blatant bid for attention. Logan complied and Dev saw the dog's back foot begin to pedal.

"Keep that up and you'll have a friend for life."

Logan's shoulders wilted and Dev mentally kicked himself. Jenna had said the children's mother had only rented the cabin for the summer. And something in Jenna's expression had told Dev that she hoped it wouldn't be that long.

"I heard Aunt Jenna tell Miss Eversea that she wants us to move in with her when Mom gets out of the hospital." Logan's voice dropped to a whisper, as if he were afraid someone might hear him. "I don't want to leave again. I like it here."

"Maybe your mom will want to stay."

Dev had meant the words to be an encouragement, but Logan seemed to deflate even more. "I
should probably go. Now that I know you're okay
and everything."

Violet nudged his hand, sensing the change in
her friend's mood. Logan sneaked one last, longing glance at the campfire before he trudged away.

You're a marshmallow, Dev. A marsh. Mallow.

Jenna had made it clear she didn't want her
nephew to get attached to Violet, but at the moment Dev went with his gut. And his gut said the
kid could use a friend.

"Have you eaten supper yet?"

Logan paused. Cast a quick, hopeful look over
one shoulder. "No."

"Well, Violet and I can't eat all these hamburgers by ourselves." Not entirely true, but it wouldn't
hurt them to share. "You're welcome to join us."

"Really?" Logan perked up like a dandelion
after a summer shower.

"Really. But you have to—"

"Ask Aunt Jenna." Logan was already halfway
to the woods. "I will. I'll be right back."

Violet's tail began to beat the ground as her
friend disappeared.

Dev glanced down at her, already regretting the
impulsive invitation.

Not because he'd changed *his* mind, but because
Jenna wouldn't.

Chapter Six

Someone needed to be confined to the cabin.

At the moment, Jenna wasn't sure whether it should be her nephew or her neighbor's dog!

She'd had a long talk with Logan about staying in the yard where she could see him, but several times over the past few days she'd caught him following Violet down the shoreline or into the woods.

Ever since Kate had given Logan the hat she'd found on a shelf in the utility closet and nicknamed him Daniel Boone, Logan had spent the better part of the day pretending to be the famous explorer.

Jenna took one more lap around the yard in case she'd missed him. There was no sign of her nephew—or the furry Pied Piper who'd led him astray.

"Let's take a walk and find Logan," Jenna told Tori, trying not to let her anxiety show.

"Okay." Tori didn't seem the least bit concerned about her brother's absence.

As they started down the overgrown path between the two cabins, a sudden, unwelcome thought traced a cold finger down Jenna's spine. What if Logan hadn't followed Violet home? What if he'd gone exploring on his own and somehow gotten lost?

She quickened her pace, dodging the roots that protruded from the ground and the branches that reached out to snag her clothing.

"There he is!" Tori pointed down the trail.

Relief washed through Jenna when she saw a small boy chugging toward them.

Logan's face lit with a smile as they approached. Until Tori planted both hands on her hips and thrust out her chin.

"Where've you been? Aunt Jenna was worried about you."

Logan peeked up at Jenna. What he saw on her face must have confirmed that his sister spoke the truth because the smile disappeared.

"I'm sorry," he mumbled.

Jenna drew in a slow breath and held it for several seconds until her pulse evened out. "Logan, you promised you wouldn't leave the yard, remember?"

"I know, but I smelled smoke. I had to make

sure Violet was okay." Logan bit his lip and Jenna felt a corresponding tug on her heart.

She might have understood his reason for disobeying one of the rules, but that didn't mean she could ignore it.

"Don't be mad at Logan. He likes to es'plore." Loyalty to her big brother prompted Tori to come to his defense. "Mom wouldn't let us play outside until she woke up and sometimes she slept *all* day."

A knot formed in Jenna's stomach. Even if it were a slight exaggeration, she tried to imagine two active children confined to a small cabin for hours on end. The more she learned about Logan and Tori's past, the more concerned she became for their future.

When Shelly returned, would their lives be different?

Jenna was beginning to think she'd been naive to assume that life would go on as usual once she returned to Minneapolis. In just a few short days, the children had not only become part of her life, they were working their way into her heart.

No matter what happened, she was determined not to let Shelly disappear again, the way she had seven years ago.

"You have to let me know your plans. I would have gone with you." Even though her heart, which held firm under the pressure of weekly deadlines and changing marketing stats, buckled at the thought of seeing Dev again.

Logan looked down at his feet and the hat slid down his forehead. "I'm sorry."

Jenna took her nephew's hand and gave it a reassuring squeeze. "We can talk about it when we get back to the cabin. I thought I'd make spaghetti for supper. How does that sound?"

"But Dev wants us to eat with him."

Jenna stared down at him. "Dev wants…he invited us over for supper?"

"He's making hamburgers."

"I like hamburgers way better than s'getti," Tori said. "I like Violet and Dev, too. Don't you, Aunt Jenna?"

Jenna rubbed her bare arms, feeling the slight chill in the air that accompanied the setting sun. A sharp contrast to the heat that flared in her cheeks in the aftermath of Tori's innocent question.

She didn't *want* to like Dev.

"I don't think that's a good idea, sweetie."

A frown puckered Logan's forehead. "Why not?"

Why not?

Looking at their expectant faces, Jenna tried to come up with an answer that would satisfy them. It was difficult, considering she couldn't think of one fast enough.

Logan took advantage of the silence to press his

advantage. "Dev cooks over the campfire every night. I think he's a real explorer."

Or a man who didn't own a cookbook.

Jenna wavered. She hadn't seen Dev for several days, but she hadn't been able to stop thinking about him, either. What did he do for a living? Where did he live? Given the fact that Logan and Violet were fast becoming inseparable, in spite of her best effort to keep them apart, it wouldn't hurt to know a little bit more about the man who lived next door.

She could get to know him…without getting to know him.

"Come on, Aunt Jenna." Tori tugged on her arm. "We can have s'getti tomorrow night."

"All right." Jenna said the words before she could change her mind. "We can't stay long, though—" She found herself talking to the trees.

"It's not far," Logan called over his shoulder as he and Tori disappeared around a bend in the trail.

Jenna followed at a slower pace, wondering what she'd gotten herself into.

Why had Dev invited them for a meal? Especially after she'd rebuffed his offer to let Logan fish off his dock the last time they'd spoken.

Jenna had told Dev a half-truth when she'd claimed that she didn't want Logan to get attached to the place. She was more worried that her nephew would get attached to Dev.

Jenna had been absent from Logan and Tori's life for the last seven years, but she was determined to do everything she could to protect them from disappointment.

Logan was lonely. It would be all too easy for him to begin to rely on Dev and then have to face the pain of another goodbye.

Too easy for her, too.

The trees thinned out and opened to a clearing. Jenna caught up to the children, who'd stopped to wait for her.

She wasn't sure what she expected to find on the other side of the woods. Maybe something as old and dilapidated as the cabin they were living in.

"Pretty." Tori summed it up in one word and Jenna couldn't help but nod in agreement.

A log home with a wraparound deck overlooking the lake and a fieldstone chimney blended seamlessly into its surroundings. A flagstone path wound down to the water. There was no formal landscaping, only a colorful patchwork quilt of wildflowers and grasses native to the area.

Dev had his back to them as he knelt beside a stone fire pit. Curls of gray smoke drifted into the air and hung low in the branches of the trees like Spanish moss.

"I'm back!" Logan shouted.

Dev turned around and the stunned look on

his face made Jenna wonder if Logan had made a mistake.

"Logan, are you sure Dev invited all three of us over for supper?" she said in a terse whisper.

"He has lots of hamburgers. He said so."

But that didn't answer her question.

Jenna's heart flipped over as Dev rose fluidly to his feet. How was it possible for a man to look so good in a pair of faded jeans, a plain cotton T-shirt and hiking boots?

"I think there's been—" *Another opportunity to embarrass herself!* "—a misunderstanding." Jenna realized she was stammering. She *never* stammered.

Dev didn't answer.

Jenna tried again. "Logan said you invited us over for supper."

"I did."

"Oh." Jenna felt her pulse even out. "It's just that you looked...surprised...to see us."

Surprised wasn't quite the word Dev would have chosen to describe his reaction when Jenna stepped into the clearing, wearing a filmy blue dress that hugged her slender curves and showed off her tanned limbs to perfection.

Shocked was more like it.

When a few minutes had ticked by and Logan hadn't returned, Dev figured it would be dinner for one again. He'd shaken off an annoying pinch of disappointment and told himself that it was probably for the best. No doubt Jenna had already labeled him a hick, complete with an unruly dog and a cabin in the woods. No sense adding to the stereotype by cooking her supper over an open fire.

If he and Jenna had met a few years ago, he would have reserved the best table at an exclusive restaurant. Dropped the names of a few important people over a gourmet meal. Charmed his way through her defenses.

Dev wondered what Jenna would say if he told her that his family owned one of the most successful companies in the Midwest and that he'd been second in the line of succession?

You're wasting your life here.

That's what Elaina had said. She'd never understood that he'd *found* his life when he moved to Mirror Lake.

Dev tore his gaze away from Jenna. He wasn't out to impress his neighbor or anyone else. Not anymore.

"Have a seat." Dev offered her the only chair in front of the fire.

Jenna flicked a dubious glance at the strip of canvas stretched over a rickety metal skeleton and remained standing. Just in case he'd forgotten why he didn't entertain.

"The other option is one of those." Dev pointed to one of the oak logs that doubled as seating until they became firewood.

Jenna chose the chair, her stiff posture and serious expression more suited for a board meeting than an informal barbecue.

The breeze sifted through her hair, teasing the silken strands. Coaxing her to lighten up and enjoy the beauty of a summer evening.

Suddenly tempted with the same thought, Dev shoved his hands in the front pockets of his jeans.

Eyes on the fire, McGuire.

At least the children had made themselves at home. Tori hopscotched her way down the crooked path from stone to stone while Logan chased Violet around the yard.

Leaving the adults stranded in an uncomfortable silence.

Jenna looked him straight in the eye. "You can tell me the truth now. Was this your idea? Or Logan's?"

"I'm the guilty one."

"No hints?"

"No hints." Dev didn't count the longing look Logan had cast at the campfire.

"I don't know what to do." Jenna sighed. "Logan promised he wouldn't leave the yard, but I'm afraid nothing can compete with dogs and campfires."

"I've been trying to keep Violet close to home,

but because no one has lived in your cabin for years, she considers it part of her territory." Dev swung the metal grate on the tripod over the fire and adjusted the height for cooking. It was easier to concentrate when he kept his hands busy and his eyes off the beautiful woman sitting beside him.

"It isn't safe for Logan to keep wandering off." Frustration stitched the words together.

"He came over because he smelled the smoke."

"I know." Jenna shook her head. "I'm not sure how I can scold him for caring about someone."

"It must be difficult to lay down the law when you're used to being the cool aunt, not the parent."

Jenna didn't comment. So much for his amateur psychology skills.

Dev was about to put her mind at ease and tell her that he'd be leaving for a few days—and taking Violet with him—when a high-pitched scream drowned out the crackle of the fire.

Dev's head whipped around. Both children were barreling toward them, short legs pumping, arms outstretched, ready to grab on to the closest port in the storm.

Which happened to be the two adults standing by the campfire.

Dev didn't hesitate. He scooped Tori up in his arms while Logan clung to Jenna, his face bleached of color.

The little girl was trembling so violently, Dev could feel the vibrations down to his toes. "Hey now," he murmured. "What happened?"

"A bee!" Tori wailed.

"Did it sting you?" Dev was already searching for any telltale welts rising on her bare arms.

"It *looked* at me!" Tori buried her face against his shoulder.

Dev's eyes met Jenna's over the little girl's head and something in her expression warned him not to smile.

"I don't see the bee anymore." He kept his voice calm. "It must have flown away."

"Did Violet get stinged?" Tori whispered.

Since the dog was stretched out in the grass, dismantling another tennis ball, Dev could only guess she was fine.

"See for yourself."

Tori peered over his shoulder and her grip around his neck relaxed, allowing Dev to breathe again. Until he tried to set her down.

"I don't like bees." Unshed tears spiked the golden lashes.

Dev glanced at Jenna, who looked almost as pale as Logan.

"I was just about to put the burgers on," he said slowly. "But I need a helper to put the cheese on top. It's a very special job." Dev tipped his head and gave Tori a thoughtful look. "What do you think? Can you help me out?"

A single tear rolled down a plump cheek, followed by a sniffle. "Uh-huh."

"Great." *Great.* "And Logan? I need two more logs from the woodpile over there. Let Violet carry one." Dev winked at him. "It makes her feel important."

Logan summoned a tremulous smile and detached himself from Jenna's side. He patted his leg to get the dog's attention. "Come on, Violet."

Dev carried Tori over to the picnic table and eased her onto the bench. Jenna sat down beside her, which gave Dev a moment to check on Logan's progress.

Five minutes later, their tasks completed and the bee momentarily forgotten, the children ran off to play again.

"Thank you," Jenna murmured.

"For what?"

She looked surprised that he had to ask. "For... understanding."

"I wouldn't go that far," Dev admitted. "But it was obvious they were scared. You don't make light of that." He paused. "Spiders, on the other hand, now those are a different story."

Just as he'd hoped, a faint smile tugged at the corners of Jenna's lips. "And wolves?"

"Definitely wolves."

Jenna spread her hands over the flames, absorbing the heat. She didn't look at him.

"Logan and Tori stirred up a nest of hornets last week," she finally said. "Both of them were stung multiple times."

Dev's stomach clenched. That explained the strong reaction. Ground hornets had a reputation for being territorial and aggressive. He'd had the misfortune to stumble on a nest once and it wasn't something a person forgot in a hurry.

"That must have been pretty traumatic. Were you with them at the time?"

"No, it happened the day I arrived in Mirror Lake. Alex Porter, Abby O'Halloran's brother, managed to get them to safety, but he's allergic to bees. Logan and Tori saw him collapse."

Dev expelled a slow breath, choosing his next words with care. "They've been through a lot, haven't they?"

Jenna flinched. Wrapped her arms around her middle in an attempt to ward off the chill. Or his questions. "Alex is all right now, but I think Logan and Tori still blame themselves."

"And you blame yourself for not being there."

Jenna didn't say anything, but then again, she didn't have to.

Dev had seen that expression before.

Every time he looked in the mirror.

Chapter Seven

Jenna felt the warmth of Dev's gaze like a physical touch.

She couldn't admit that in a way, she was to blame for the children's traumatic collision with the hornets that day. Logan and Tori had hidden in an old car on the property next to the bed-and-breakfast because they'd been running away from *her.*

Grace had tried to explain that children living in "family situations" similar to theirs had a tendency to be leery of people they didn't know, but that had only made Jenna feel worse.

In her niece's and nephew's eyes, she was a stranger.

Understanding the children's reaction to her arrival in Mirror Lake didn't make it any easier to bear.

Jenna still couldn't believe her sister had never

talked about her. Told Logan and Tori they had an aunt. That's what hurt the most. As close as she and Shelly had been as children, it was if Jenna had never existed.

"Are *you* okay?"

With a start, Jenna realized Dev was studying her, the golden-brown eyes intent on her face.

"I'm fine." If she kept saying it, maybe she would eventually begin to believe it.

"The burgers will be ready to flip in about ten minutes. How are you at cutting up fruit?"

"I think I can manage."

"Then follow me." Dev started toward the cabin and Jenna struggled to keep up with his loose-limbed stride.

"Wait a second." A thought suddenly occurred to her. "You wouldn't be trying to distract me the way you distracted Tori and Logan?"

"I have no idea what you're talking about."

"Uh-huh." Jenna shot him a suspicious look.

As they reached the short flight of steps leading up to the deck, Dev paused. Rubbed a hand across his jaw as he looked at the sky.

"Come to think of it, it did work, though, didn't it?" he mused.

"Yes." Jenna rolled her eyes, even though she had to admit Dev handled the crisis better than she did when Tori and Logan had started screaming.

In her column, Jenna taught women how to protect everything from their dry-clean-only knits to their investment portfolios. Dealing with Tori's recurring nightmares and Logan's overdeveloped sense of responsibility was beyond her realm of experience.

For a split second, Jenna had the overwhelming urge to rest her cheek against Dev's broad shoulder with complete trust, the way Tori had, and tell him everything.

Jenna's hands fisted at her sides.

What was she thinking? Trusting people only led to disappointment. Trusting a man she'd met a few days ago was downright crazy.

"We'll take the shortcut." Dev bounded up the short flight up steps to the deck that jutted out in a V-shape from the front of the cabin. "You'll be able to watch the kids from the window."

When he opened the sliding glass door, Jenna could see what he meant.

Floor to ceiling glass provided a frame for the spectacular sunset over the lake. Vaulted ceilings lined with knotty pine boards added a warm, natural glow to the open floor plan.

The mismatched furnishings had been chosen with an eye for comfort rather than style. A rawhide leather sofa, worn from use, faced a massive stone fireplace that took up an entire wall. There was no television, only a stack of books on the coffee table and a telescope on a tripod in the corner. All in all, the cabin had a certain rugged appeal.

Like the man who lived there.

Jenna set that thought firmly to the side.

For years, she had clipped out pictures from magazines and catalogs and saved them in a folder. Her condo was a collage of those dreams. Simple but stylish furnishings. The walls a pale gray, the trim board tangerine. Open cupboards in the tiled kitchen displayed a set of dishes, white with a splash of black in the center. Chic. Trendy.

Even if Jenna couldn't remember the last time she'd invited someone over for dinner.

"Not much to look at, is it?" Dev's tone sounded more affectionate than critical.

"It's…cozy." Jenna's gaze lingered on the fireplace.

Before she could prevent the scene in her mind from unfolding, Jenna suddenly saw herself sitting on the sofa in front of a roaring fire, cradled in butter soft leather.

And Dev's arms.

She gripped the back of the sofa, her fingers curling into the flannel blanket draped over its wooden spine.

Where had *that* come from?

Mirror Lake hadn't even made the "Thirty Places Every Girl Should Visit Before She Turns

Thirty" that Jenna had highlighted in her column the previous month.

An isolated, lakeside cabin wasn't on the list, either. And it certainly had never been part of her dreams.

Neither was a man like Dev.

A man who remained blissfully ignorant of the battle raging inside of her as he rummaged through a drawer in the kitchen.

"Have you lived here a long time?" Jenna managed to find her voice again.

"My grandfather bought this place after the Depression. He called it his fishing cabin." Dev's muffled voice drifted toward her. "I spent a few weeks with him every summer but I never saw him do any actual fishing. The only thing I remember seeing him do was sleep in the hammock all afternoon."

Jenna frowned. "I assumed you grew up in Mirror Lake."

"Really." A bag of apples landed on the countertop. "What makes you say that? The flannel shirt you're tying into knots—"

Horrified, Jenna looked down and saw a neat little placket of tortoiseshell buttons on what she'd thought was a throw.

"—or the 'I Love My Truck' poster on the wall?"

"You don't have any posters on your wall." She'd looked. "And you drive an SUV."

"Violet picked it out. She doesn't know the difference." Dev's crooked smile took her heart for a spin.

Feeling a little lightheaded, Jenna smiled back.

The refrigerator door swung open, blocking Dev from view. She continued the conversation anyway. Because really, he'd started it.

"It's just that you seem comfortable here." Comfortable in his own skin. "You...fit in."

"Is that so?"

Even though she couldn't see the smile on his face, she heard it in his voice. This time, however, Jenna had the impression he was laughing at himself, not at her.

What was wrong with fitting in?

It was something Jenna had always wanted. Moving from town to town at her mother's whim made it difficult to put down roots. Or make friends. She'd dreamed of having a room of her own. A real home.

We're here to stay, Nola would promise. And then a few months later, they would pack up and move again. It wasn't until college that Jenna had been able to reinvent herself.

No one knew about her past so Jenna was finally able to embrace her future. To make her own dreams come true.

The fact that she'd succeeded had surprised Jenna most of all.

"Pickings are kind of slim right now." Dev tossed a twiggy branch of shriveled grapes to the growing pile of fruit on the counter. "I've been gone a lot."

Dev didn't say why, but it was the opening Jenna had hoped for.

"What do you do—" A framed photograph on the coffee table caught Jenna's eye. She moved closer for a better look.

Through a veil of pouring rain, a mother eagle perched on the edge of a nest, one enormous wing stretched over three eaglets huddled together, sound asleep.

Jenna's breath caught in her throat. "This photograph is incredible."

Behind the refrigerator door came a muffled grunt.

"It looks like the mother eagle is protecting her babies from the storm," Jenna murmured. "How would a photographer even know to *wait* for a shot like this?"

"Sometimes a person is in the right place at the right time."

Jenna frowned at Dev's back. Didn't he realize how amazing it was?

She leaned closer and noticed a small inscription in the corner. "Do you know what this means? Psalm 91:4?"

All sound in the kitchen ceased.

Dev rose from behind the breakfast bar to look at her now. "It's a verse from the Bible."

"I know that." Jenna cast him an impatient look. Her friend, Caitlin, included a passage from the same book underneath the IMAGEine logo. "Have you ever looked it up? Do you know what it *says?*"

Dev was staring at her with such an odd expression that Jenna wished she hadn't asked.

"He will cover you with his feathers, and under his wings you will find refuge."

Something in the husky timbre of his voice told Jenna that not only could Dev quote the verse, he *believed* it.

Jenna was staring at him now, not the photograph.

Dev braced himself, waiting for her to mock the words. Or worse yet, dismiss them as irrelevant. Elaina had. He couldn't blame her. He'd done the same thing to Jason every chance he got. It was a wonder his brother could stand to be in the same room with him, let alone seek out his company.

"It's a nice thought." There was not a hint of sarcasm in the words. Only…longing?

Dev didn't know what to say. He was no preacher. Most of the time, he wasn't sure if he was even getting this faith stuff right. He only knew that his life had been irrevocably changed five years ago.

"It's more than a nice thought," Dev heard himself say. "It's true."

He waited for Jenna to retreat the way she had when he'd tried to find out more about Logan and Tori. Or laugh at him. Instead, she touched the frame, her expression almost wistful.

"How do you know?"

"Because…" Dev felt his throat tighten. He couldn't answer Jenna's question without telling her about Jason and he wasn't ready for that. Not yet. It was a wound slow to heal; one he'd kept covered. "I've experienced it."

"An invisible umbrella?" The wistful expression in her eyes disappeared, snuffed out by a shadow of skepticism. "I know a lot of people who've been caught in a downpour that would disagree with you."

And Jenna was one of them.

Really, God? Dev sent a silent complaint heavenward. *I remembered the story about the Good Samaritan. Invited my neighbors over for dinner. Now you want me to tell Jenna about you?*

Jason would have known exactly what to say.

"God doesn't promise there won't be storms." Dev gave it a shot. "He promises not to leave us alone in the midst of them."

Jenna's eyebrows dipped together as if he were speaking a language she didn't understand.

The fragile connection between them was broken as the door swung open and Logan poked his head in. "Dev? The burgers are making lotsa smoke."

Jenna looked as grateful for the interruption as he was.

"I'll stay here." She reached for the bag of apples and the paring knife he'd set on the counter.

"Sounds good." Really good. Dev wasn't comfortable with the feelings that Jenna stirred up inside of him.

Her independence and vulnerability were proving to be a dangerous combination, testing Dev's resolve to keep his distance.

He tried to picture Jenna being content to spend her evening in an isolated cabin, watching the stars for entertainment. In Mirror Lake the closest thing to a night at the symphony was the one the crickets and frogs performed outside the window on a summer evening.

The fact that she'd dropped her guard long enough to accept his dinner invitation was probably proof that she was already bored to death.

In the interest of self-preservation, Dev followed Logan outside and stayed by the campfire until Jenna returned a few minutes later, cradling a bowl of fresh fruit in her hands.

She stopped and looked around.

"Are you missing something?" Dev slid the last burger onto a plate.

"A table?"

Smiling, Dev pointed to a wool blanket spread on the ground. "It's right there."

Logan and Tori didn't share their aunt's hesitation. They dropped to their knees on the blanket while Jenna positioned herself gingerly on one corner.

Dev might have forgotten what it was like to have company, but there was something he did remember to do before every meal.

"Do you mind if I ask a blessing?"

Logan and Tori bowed their heads. With another curious look in his direction, Jenna imitated the gesture a moment later.

Dev closed his eyes. "Lord God, thank you for today. Thank you for the beauty of your creation and for the food you've provided. Bless it to our bodies and bless the people gathered here in your presence. Amen."

"Amen," Logan and Tori repeated.

Jenna's head remained bowed a few more seconds, her gaze fixed on the table. When she looked up, Dev sucked in a breath.

Tears shimmered in her eyes.

For the first time, it occurred to him that maybe Logan wasn't the only one who needed a friend.

Jenna remained silent throughout the meal, anticipating the children's needs and encouraging them to try a bite of everything while the food on her plate remained virtually untouched.

Tori chatted about everything from the red squirrel that lived in the tree outside her bedroom window to the new clothes the mailman had delivered that morning.

Jenna smiled occasionally, but Dev couldn't help but notice a subtle change in her demeanor as they ate. One he traced back to the moment he'd quoted the passage in Psalms.

Or maybe, Dev chided himself, Jenna was simply used to more scintillating company.

Tori giggled when Violet stalked a fuzzy brown and black caterpillar through the grass. The dog was doing a better job entertaining their guests than he was.

As soon as their plates were empty, Logan and Tori ran off to play. Jenna began to clean up, a sure sign she was ready to call it a night.

Her next words confirmed it. "Thank you for supper. We should probably be getting back soon. It's getting close to Logan and Tori's bedtime."

Dev checked the fire and saw nothing left but a few glowing coals.

"I'll walk you home."

"That's not necessary," Jenna said quickly.

"No matter what you think of me, my mama raised a gentleman." She'd also made him attend weeks of etiquette classes when he was ten years old but Jenna didn't need to know that.

Tori drifted over, a bouquet of limp daisies clutched in her hand. "Can you carry me? My legs feel heavy."

She lifted up her arms.

To him.

"Jenna?"

The expression on her pretty face made it clear that he wasn't supposed to be part of her exit plan. But while she had no trouble saying no to him, Tori was another story.

It would have been easier, Jenna thought, if Dev had gone all Neanderthal and overruled her decision. But he left it up to her.

"All right." Jenna gave in. Again. A short walk and a quick thank you. She could do that.

Dev settled Tori into the crook of his arm. "We'll take the trail by the shoreline instead of through the woods this time."

Logan pressed himself against Dev's side, searching for shapes that didn't belong in the deepening shadows. "Because of the bears?"

Jenna couldn't believe that he actually sounded a little excited about the possibility.

"Worse," Dev whispered as he handed her nephew the flashlight. "Mosquitoes."

Logan's gurgle of laughter vibrated through the evening air and Jenna soaked in the sound as they set out. It wasn't often that her nephew let his guard down long enough to laugh the way a seven-year-old boy *should* laugh.

Watching him chase Violet around Dev's yard and climb imaginary mountains were good for a child who'd had too much responsibility placed on his shoulders.

Jenna knew what that felt like.

"Shhh." Dev paused for a moment and pointed to the shoreline. A doe stood at the edge of the water, her nose to the wind, velvet ears twitching.

Tori lifted her head from his shoulder and blinked, her eyes already at half-mast. "It's a deer."

"Wait," Dev whispered. He looked down at Violet and put a finger to his lips. The dog obediently settled at his feet.

A heartbeat later, two spindly legged fawns emerged from the shadows and ambled to their mother's side.

While the doe kept watch, the twins began a playful game of tag, romping through the shallow water and kicking up sand like children on a day at the beach.

Dev, who'd started out in the lead, had somehow ended up beside her. The breeze stirred the air, combining the rich texture of pine and water with a clean, masculine scent that Jenna was beginning to recognize.

She was also beginning to recognize that her

heart seemed to have its own agenda when it came to Dev. Everything in Jenna's head warned her not to get too close but her heart, always so agreeable in the past, moved toward him like the needle of a compass seeking the north pole.

That she was even thinking in those terms told her that she needed to get back to the city.

An owl hooted in a branch above their heads and the doe's tail lifted like a white flag as she bounded into the woods. The spotted fawns melted into the shadows behind her.

"Can we follow them?" Tori wanted to know.

Dev's teeth flashed in the darkness. "I think their mama is going to tuck them into bed for the night. She wouldn't want us to disturb them."

"Okay." Tori tucked her cheek against Dev's shoulder. Yawned. "Tomorrow?"

"We have plans tomorrow," Jenna interjected. She'd make sure of it.

Chapter Eight

Jenna found an empty parking spot right in front of the Grapevine Cafe the following afternoon. Her sunglasses hid the effects of a sleepless night.

Funny how she'd been able to sleep through the constant swish of traffic and sirens outside her condo but now she woke up every time a cricket chirped.

And without fail, every time her eyes had popped open, Dev had popped into her thoughts. Jenna's attention to detail, something she'd always prided herself on, had turned on her, forcing her to relive every moment spent in Dev's company the evening before.

The man was the quintessential "what you see is what you get" type of guy. No games. No apologies. He didn't flirt with her. Didn't fall all over himself trying to impress her. His quiet strength and dry wit invited a woman to let her guard down.

No wonder Logan and Tori liked him. Jenna should have been just as comfortable in his presence but somehow she ended up as jittery as a Macy's employee on Black Friday.

The jitters hadn't subsided until she loaded the children into her car and drove to the bed-and-breakfast to visit Abby for a few hours. While they were there, Kate called and asked if she and the children could stop by the cafe for a few minutes.

Jenna had welcomed another reason to avoid the cabin.

And Dev.

Logan unsnapped his seat belt and scrambled out of the car while Jenna unbuckled Tori from her booster seat.

"There you are!" The door of the cafe swung open, and Kate stepped under the striped awning, a snow-white apron tied around her trim waist.

"I have a new shirt." Tori skipped over to Kate and pointed to the pink pony decal on the front. "The mailman brought it. It's gotta sparkly mane, see?"

"It's beautiful—just like you." Kate smiled at Jenna over Tori's head and gave the tail of Logan's hat a tug. "How are you doing, buddy? Have you made any exciting discoveries yet?"

"There's something living in a hole underneath the porch."

"What do you think it is?" Kate's voice dropped to a whisper.

"I don't know but it likes crackers."

Kate chuckled. "Come on in. The midday rush is over so we should have the place to ourselves for a while."

Jenna followed Kate and the children inside and felt as if she'd stepped back in time.

Red vinyl stools with spindly metal legs lined the long counter in front of the old-fashioned soda fountain. A Beach Boys tune blared from a jukebox in the corner. In the Twin Cities, Jenna had no doubt that people would flock to the cafe to experience its "vintage" charm.

Logan and Tori bypassed the dessert carousel and aimed for a booth in front of the window.

"They seem to be doing better," Kate murmured. "Are you settling in?"

"Adjusting," Jenna admitted. "Settling in" had never been part of her plan.

Kate tipped her head to one side, a gesture Jenna was coming to recognize. "How is your sister?"

"I don't know." Jenna tried to hide her frustration. "I've left several messages for Shelly but she hasn't returned my calls. The director at New Day is on vacation and won't be back until the end of the week. I have no idea what's going on."

"I've been praying for her. And for you." Kate squeezed Jenna's hand.

"Thank you." Jenna realized that she meant it.

Dev had prayed over their meal the evening before and the simple words had touched a chord inside her.

Prayer had never been an important part of Jenna's life. No one else had paid any attention to her so she'd assumed that God didn't either. But Dev's simple prayer had echoed through a hollow space in her heart. The one that never seemed to go away, no matter how much her salary or her popularity increased.

You have it all, people would often tell her. So why did she always feel as if something were missing?

He will cover you with his feathers, and under his wings you will find refuge.

The verse cycled through her memory again and she thought about the photograph on Dev's coffee table. She'd never felt that safe. That protected...

"Okay, if you aren't going to choose, I'll just have to bring you one of each!"

Jenna snapped to attention when she realized Kate had been talking to her. "One of each?"

"I asked if you wanted a hot fudge sundae or a piece of pie." Kate chuckled. "But you were obviously somewhere else."

Jenna wasn't about to tell her where. "Sorry. I've got a lot on my mind. I'll just have a cup of coffee."

"Coffee it is." Kate ducked behind the counter. "Have a seat, and I'll be right back."

Tori and Logan were already hard at work building a tower with the tiny packets of jam on the table when Jenna slid into the booth beside them.

"Miss Gardner?"

Jenna looked up as a man maneuvered through the maze of tables toward her. The shock of red hair sprouting from the top of his head resembled a rooster's comb and matched the stripes in his plaid golf shorts.

He stuck out a hand. "I'm Wes Collins, editor of the *Mirror Lake Register*."

Jenna smiled politely. "It's nice to meet you, Mr. Collins."

"Kate tells me that you write a column for a magazine."

Jenna glanced over at Kate, who grinned and waved a spoon at her. "That's right. *Twin City Trends*."

Wes grabbed an empty chair and positioned it at the end of the table, effectively blocking off any chance of escape.

But why did Jenna have the feeling she was going to need one?

"Gabby Bunker is my best correspondent. You've probably heard of her."

"Um...no. But I haven't had a chance to read your newspaper yet."

"Oh." Wes looked disappointed. "She's having surgery next week and has to take a few weeks off."

"I'm sorry to hear that."

"The last time Gabby took a break, sales sank quicker than Charlie Pendleton's raft in the Reflection Days race."

"I'm sure she'll be difficult to replace." Jenna tried to catch Kate's eye, willing her to stage a hot fudge sundae intervention.

"Actually—" Wes leaned forward, trapping her in a cloud of Old Spice.

Oh. *No*.

"—I was wondering if you'd fill in for her. As a favor for a fellow journalist."

A fellow journalist?

"I know it sounds a little intimidating," Wes continued, his expression earnest. "I mean, Gabby gets fan mail from all over the county. People *love* her column."

"I'm sure they do." Jenna pressed her lips together to seal off a smile.

"I already talked to her and she's willing to give you a chance."

"That's very, um, nice, of her," Jenna managed. "And I appreciate the offer, Mr. Collins, but unfortunately—" Or fortunately, depending on a person's point of view "—I won't be in Mirror Lake very long. I'm sure you'd rather have someone you can depend on."

"Right." Wes's smile didn't fade as he pushed to his feet. "I'll give you some time to think about it."

Jenna blinked. Hadn't she already thought about it? And said no?

"Mr. Collins—"

"Call me Wes. All the other correspondents do. We're like one big happy family down at the *Register*."

Jenna wanted to make it clear that she wasn't—nor did she intend to be—one of his correspondents, but the door was already closing behind him.

Kate returned and divvied up the sundaes between Logan and Tori. She set a generous slice of pie down in front of Jenna.

"Compliments of Wes."

"He's trying to bribe me. With pie."

"It's worked before."

"Did you put him up to this?" Jenna had heard Abby tease Kate about her "recruiting" skills.

"I might have mentioned you wrote for a magazine." Kate didn't look the least bit repentant.

"A *lifestyle* magazine."

"Hey." Kate's chin shot up but laughter danced in her green eyes. "We have a lifestyle here, too, you know. It's just a little—"

"Slower?"

"Slower isn't always a bad thing."

"Kate, you know I don't plan to be here very long."

The cafe owner didn't look put off by Jenna's statement. In fact, she had the audacity to wink at her.

"Sometimes God has other plans."

There were two messages waiting for Dev on his answering machine when he walked in the door.

The first one he ignored, the second one he couldn't. Not if he wanted to keep Violet in kibbles and rawhide chews.

He hit a button on his speed dial and waited, hoping it would go straight to voice mail.

"It's about time!"

No such luck. "Hey, Talia."

"Hi, yourself. You know, just to bring you up to speed on the latest technology, there are these handy little things called cell phones that make communication a lot easier."

"Ah, but they were designed for people who *want* to communicate."

"You take this whole backwoods hermit thing a little too seriously."

"I'm not a hermit."

A brief moment of silence and then, "'A hermit. One that retires from society and lives in solitude.' That's a quote straight from Mr. Webster that I found on my BlackBerry. One of those handy gadgets I referred to a moment ago, not the actual berry."

"You know service around here can be sketchy."

"Mmm, that's what you keep telling me, but sometimes I wonder if it's a convenient excuse."

Dev poured a cup of coffee—a conversation with Talia Hunt always called for caffeine—and tossed a biscuit to Violet. "Is this a business call or an 'I think Dev needs another lecture' call?"

An exasperated sigh unfurled in his ear. "It's a 'remind me why I put up with you' call."

Dev grinned. He could picture Talia's ebony braids trembling like aspen leaves; hear the indignant scuff of her Birkenstocks as she paced the length of a glass wall overlooking the Mississippi.

The gallery Talia owned was located in an old warehouse a group of artists had rescued from demolition. She and Jason had been friends, which in Talia's mind meant that *they* were friends. A sneaky tactic she'd used to stay in touch with him the past few years.

"I was planning to call you. I just got home a few days ago."

"And?"

And I've been distracted by the new neighbors. Dev kept that information to himself. Even a crusty old hermit had a reputation to live up to.

"I might have gotten one or two decent shots." Dev propped a hip against the counter and looked out the window. The thick stand of trees blocked his view of Jenna's cabin, but through the screen he heard a peal of childish laughter and a loud splash.

He'd heard the purr of her Audi a few hours ago, heading toward town.

Violet, who'd been moping around for the better part of the day, trotted over to the sliding glass door and whined.

"Forget about it," Dev told her.

"But you just said—"

"Sorry. I was talking to Violet."

"I rest my case." Talia sounded smug. "Let me know when I can drive to Mirror Lake and pick up the photos. Unless you feel like taking a trip into town, Mr. Ingalls."

"Or I could mail them."

"Violet and I like to catch up."

And Talia liked to check on him.

"I'll let you know. *Soon.*" Dev added the word before she could ask.

"If you'd agree to make more than one copy of a photo, I wouldn't have to bother you so often."

"We've had this conversation."

"And it's one of my favorites."

"Then you may recall—"

"You're capturing one moment in time," Talia

interrupted. "I know, I know. One moment, one photo. I still can't decide whether it's creative genius or a brilliant marketing strategy."

Dev didn't think it was either one. A few months after he'd moved to Mirror Lake, he'd given Talia one of his photos as a gift on her birthday, something Jason would have done if he had been there.

A customer had noticed it hanging on the wall of Talia's office and wanted to buy a copy. When Talia had called to ask if he'd be interested, Dev had politely refused.

Not in a million years would he have guessed it would spark the patron's interest even more. Talia had kept at him until Dev had finally given her permission to sell some of his photos through the gallery—with the condition that each would be one of a kind.

Dev figured that would be the end of it. It was ironic that his attempt to avoid attention had backfired. With that first sale, demand for his photographs had risen, along with the price.

Talia might give him a hard time but she, more than anyone else, understood his aversion to the limelight. Dev had courted it once, never realizing what it would cost him.

"I'm going out again in a few days," Dev said, knowing it would make her happy. "There's a litter of coyote pups I've been keeping an eye on."

He frowned at Violet, whose whine had begun

to rise in volume and intensity. He gave in and opened the door. "Don't wander off."

Talia cleared her throat. "One of my customers suggested you compile your photographs into a book."

Dev watched Violet hurtle across the lawn as if she'd been shot out of a cannon. He had no trouble guessing her destination. "Bye, Talia."

"Are you avoiding the issue or do you have a date?"

An image of Jenna's face flashed in Dev's mind and he deliberately set it aside. There was no way he could label the evening they'd spent together a date. Even though he hadn't been able to stop thinking about it. Or Jenna.

"I have a dog…or at least I *had* one. She just ran away."

"Fine. But if you don't call me back by the end of next week, I'll be showing up at your door."

"Thanks for the warning." Dev shook his head and hung up the phone.

There was no sign of Violet.

As he followed her footprints down the shoreline, Dev pictured a kennel next to the garage. There'd been no need for one in the past, but Jenna had made no secret of the fact that she wasn't a dog person…

Dev heard a shriek.

Wolf? Spider? Broken nail?

He crossed the property line in time to see Logan and Tori charge around the cabin.

Only Violet wasn't the one in hot pursuit this time.

Jenna was.

Chapter Nine

At least, Dev *thought* it was Jenna.

He wasn't quite sure, given the fact that this woman was barefoot. A ponytail streamed behind her like a flag. The bright pink tank top she wore matched the color in her cheeks and faded denim shorts showed off her tanned, sculpted legs to perfection.

She was also armed with a squirt gun the size of a small cannon.

Logan spotted him first and skidded to a stop. "Hi, Dev!"

Tori collided with her brother, who collided with Jenna. All three fell down in a tangle of limbs.

Dev waded into the fray, grabbing hold of Violet's collar before she could join in.

Jenna rolled to her feet, breathless. A smile shimmered in her eyes, reminding him of the play of sunlight on water.

"What's going on?" Dev managed to find his voice.

"We're painting my room." Tori giggled.

"I thought painting involved a brush." Dev lifted a brow at Jenna.

A deeper rose shaded Jenna's already flushed cheeks. "We finished a little while ago. The paint has to dry before we can move everything back."

"We're cleaning up now," Logan said.

Dev eyed the squirt gun tucked under Jenna's arm. "Most people use the shower."

"It was Aunt Jenna's idea." Logan picked himself up off the grass. "She said this would be more fun."

"We have another squirt gun if you want to play," Tori offered. "You can be on Aunt Jenna's team."

Dev jerked as a stream of cold water hit his foot. He traced it to the barrel of Jenna's squirt gun.

"Sorry," she gasped. "I didn't mean to pull the trigger."

Dev had no doubt it was a response to Tori's innocent invitation but he let her off the hook. "Actually, I came over to get Violet."

At the sound of her name, the dog's soggy tail began to wag. Dev gave her a stern "we'll talk about this later" look.

Tori's face fell. "Don't you want to see my room first?"

"Ah…" Dev glanced at Jenna, who was swiping

at the wet blades of grass clinging to her knees. No help there.

"It's pink," Tori added, as if the color might sway Dev's decision.

Coupled with a heart-melting smile, it did.

"I'd love to," Dev heard himself say. "If it's all right with your aunt."

"Of course." Jenna summoned a smile so polite Dev wondered if she'd taken etiquette classes, too.

They trooped into the cabin and Dev tried to hide his reaction. Space-wise, it was half the size of his. The outdated colors and scuffed flooring evidence that the owner had lost interest in making improvements at least two decades ago. But the woodwork glowed and a hand-hooked wool rug anchored a pair of lumpy chairs, the hem of their tweed skirts peeking out below the crocheted afghans tucked into the cushions. Colorful silk scarves hung in the windows like sun catchers.

Jenna had claimed they wouldn't be staying in Mirror Lake very long, and yet she'd taken the time to transform a dreary cabin into a home.

Dev turned just in time to catch Jenna wringing a drop of water from the end of her ponytail.

There'd been a bit of transformation in her, too.

Jenna waited for Dev to make a teasing comment about the decor.

He smiled instead. A slow smile that made Jenna forget he'd caught her tearing around the yard dressed in one of Shelly's outfits. The end of her ponytail dripping water like the kitchen faucet.

"I like what you've done with the place."

He capped off the statement with a wink that robbed Jenna of her ability to speak.

Fortunately, Tori took command of the situation, taking Dev by the hand and leading him toward the narrow doorway of the bedroom, where the smell of paint thickened the air.

Jenna fled to her room in the opposite direction to change clothes. She shed the shorts and tank top and pulled a sundress over her head. On her way to the door, she caught a glimpse of herself in the full-length mirror on the wall. Barefoot. No makeup. Her hair a damp rope between her shoulder blades.

If her coworkers at the magazine saw her now, they wouldn't recognize her. She looked nothing like the picture of the woman in the upper right-hand corner of her column.

At the moment, she didn't *feel* like her, either.

Which, Jenna told herself, had nothing to do with the glint of admiration she'd seen in Dev's eyes when he'd accidentally crashed their post-painting cleanup party.

When she returned a few minutes later, Dev was sitting on the floor with Logan, carefully setting up a herd of yellow buffalo that had come with the frontier town Jenna had purchased at the variety store. Tori crouched inside a chuck wagon fashioned from chair cushions, pretending to pour tea into dainty plastic cups.

On the coffee table, a dozen plastic horses grazed on the cover of Jenna's expensive laptop, their riders keeping watch on the herd of plastic buffalo below.

"Come play with us, Aunt Jenna!" Tori patted an empty space on the rug. Six inches from Dev. Who appeared totally at ease sandwiched between the children and the enormous dog wedged between the chairs.

Panicked, Jenna's gaze snagged Dev's. "Play?" she choked.

"Dev said he could stay for a few minutes."

That's what she got for leaving them alone. Jenna could imagine Logan and Tori begging him not to leave. Dev wasn't immune to the power of two pairs of beseeching blue eyes.

And neither was she, as it turned out.

Jenna sat down on the rug, careful to leave a few inches of space between her and Dev. Not easy when his presence filled the room like sunlight.

"Well howdy, ma'am." Dev's Midwestern accent melted into a lazy drawl as he tipped the brim of an imaginary cowboy hat. "We hear you've been having a problem with rustlers."

"Rustlers?" Jenna repeated the word cautiously.

"They're the bad guys," Logan explained. "If they scare the buffalo, they'll stampede."

"That's bad?" Three pairs of eyes stared at her in disbelief, leaving Jenna with no choice but to rephrase the question. "That's bad. Very bad."

"Sure is, ma'am." Dev didn't crack a smile. "Because it appears your cabin—" He nodded toward a tiny log house at the foot of the chair. "Is smack-dab in the way."

Everyone was looking at her again.

"Oh, no." Jenna saw Dev shake his head and tried again. "Oh, *no!* Save my cabin. And my—" She peered down at the tiny homestead she'd recently inherited and saw a plastic farm animal grazing in what looked to be her front yard. "Peacock?"

"Chicken." Dev, Logan and Tori said the word at the same time.

Well. She was trying.

Logan puffed up his chest. "What's the plan, Marshal?"

Dev opened his mouth to speak but Jenna interrupted. "Am I a marshal?"

"Nope." Logan reached for another cowboy. "Me an' Dev are the marshals."

"And I'm the cook!" Tori announced.

"Then what am I?"

"You're the city slicker with the green peacock," Dev murmured.

Jenna was about to protest, out of principal, when Logan patted her hand. "Don't worry, ma'am. You can hide in the well and we'll take care of these ornery varmints."

"Ornery varmints?" Jenna mouthed the words at Dev.

"The rustlers." He pointed to a line of cowboys hiding in the folds of an afghan.

"Oh, right…thank you, Marshal Logan." Jenna clapped a hand over her heart. "I've been so worried about my…chicken."

With what could only be described as a swagger, Logan moved his cowboy into the path of the buffalo.

Jenna picked up her tiny plastic heroine and tucked her inside the cabin. "I'm not hiding in the well. And just so we're clear," she muttered. "I would never wear this shade of red."

Dev's low laugh rippled through her. "You're doing good. For a city slicker."

They might have been playing a game, but Jenna felt tears prick the back of her eyes.

She constantly second-guessed herself when it came to the children. Watching Tori and Logan the night before, listening to their laughter, made her realize that that she needed to interject some more fun into their lives.

She might not have known that if she hadn't accepted Dev's dinner invitation.

Jenna wasn't used to this kind of imaginary play. Growing up, she had escaped by writing down her thoughts in a journal, never entertaining the possibility that it would eventually turn into a career until Miss Franklin, one of her high school English teachers, had encouraged her to write an essay for a scholarship.

Her idea of fun was curling up on the sofa with a bowl of popcorn and watching the Style channel.

"Everything okay, ma'am?" Dev was watching her closely.

Jenna tossed her head. "Don't you have some rustlers to catch, Marshal?"

Dev retaliated with a playful tug on the end of her ponytail, as if she were Tori's age. "Yes, ma'am."

"Look out! Rock slide!" Tori shrieked.

Styrofoam packing peanuts began to tumble down the cushion and onto the rug.

"We have to stop it." Logan looked around and grabbed the first thing he saw. Jenna's latest copy of *Twin City Trends*. He tossed it to Dev, who used it as a shield to staunch the flow of rocks into the canyon.

"It worked." Logan tossed his coonskin cap into the air.

Dev wasn't celebrating their victory. He was staring at the cover of the magazine. The headline promised to share the "five favorite hangouts of the city's most famous faces" with readers.

Jenna nudged him with her elbow.

"Are you a subscriber?" she teased.

"Are you?"

"In a way. I work there."

"You work for *Twin City Trends*."

"That's right. Have you heard of it?"

The smile had faded, replaced by something that looked like disgust.

"Unfortunately."

Chapter Ten

Disappointment left a bitter taste in Dev's mouth.

Half of every issue was devoted to a certain kind of lifestyle, the other half dispensing advice on how to achieve it.

Elaina had lived her life between the covers of that magazine. She dressed like the models. Dined at the four-star restaurants reviewed every month in the foodie section. Shopped at the exclusive boutiques advertised on the glossy pages.

"It's not what you're thinking." Jenna smoothed out a wrinkled corner, collateral damage from the avalanche.

"I'm not thinking anything."

One golden brow lifted, a sure sign that Jenna didn't believe him. "*Twin City Trends* is a reputable publication. No UFO sightings or three-headed cows. We give people tips on how to live better lives."

She was *defending* it. But in all fairness, it wasn't just the magazine that Dev was struggling with. It was the reminder that Jenna didn't belong here.

She didn't belong with *him*.

"I should go." Dev rolled to his feet, careful not to take out the miniature stagecoach parked next to one of the cardboard buildings.

"But you just got here." Tori hugged Princess against her chest.

"Are you having another campfire tonight?"

Dev heard disappointment in each heavy footstep as Logan trailed him to the door.

"Not this evening, bud. I have other plans." Like getting his head on straight again. "Come on, Violet. Time to go."

The dog, who could hear a chipmunk half a mile away, ignored him.

"We can bring her over later," Logan offered.

"It'll be easier if I take her home with me now." *Easier for who,* an inner voice mocked.

"But—"

"Logan." Jenna put her hand on her nephew's shoulder, a gentle reminder not to push. "We still have to move Tori's things back into the room now that the paint is dry."

Guilt seared Dev's conscious. "Do you need some help?"

"No, thank you." Jenna shook her head, her

smile polite but guarded. Nothing like the one Dev had seen on her face a few minutes ago when she'd been transplanted into the Wild West.

Logan dropped to his knees and hugged Violet. "I have to go to church tomorrow morning but maybe I'll see you after that. We can look for crayfish."

The dog lifted her paw to shake on the deal.

"What do you say we go exploring after supper?" Dev heard Jenna say as the screen door snapped shut behind him.

He decided to take the road home to distract Violet, who shadowed him like a little dark raincloud of gloom, reminding him that the afternoon had been a lot more fun until he showed up.

"Go find something to chew up," Dev told her.

Violet growled.

Startled by the unexpected response, Dev looked down at the dog. But her gaze was fixed on a man standing under the trees several yards away.

"Can I help you?"

Dev heard a muffled curse. The guy pivoted, fists clenching at his sides. He spotted Violet and suddenly remembered his manners.

"Naw, I was just taking a walk." The man twitched when Violet padded toward him. "It's a nice day. Pretty hot, though."

Especially when you were wearing black from head to toe, Dev wanted to say.

The guy didn't look familiar, but that wasn't unusual, considering that Dev didn't go out of his way to meet the locals.

"This is private property," Dev pointed out.

"Sorry, man." The guy smirked. "I didn't know that. I saw something interesting and took a little detour."

Violet's lips pulled back in a snarl. Dev felt the same way.

"Well, now you know."

"No problem. Take it easy." He sauntered away, the hems of his black jeans leaving a trail in the dirt.

Dev waited until he passed Jenna's driveway before continuing on his way. A few seconds later, a car rumbled past him.

The driver flicked a cigarette out the open window and it landed at Dev's feet. There was no mistaking the shaggy-haired man at the wheel. Dev would have gotten a plate number, but there was a ragged hole in the spot where the license plate should have been.

The guy had told him he was going for a walk. What? To his car?

Dev's eyes narrowed on the vehicle as it disappeared around a corner.

The sun was still shining and the birds were

still singing, but something didn't feel right anymore. Dev backtracked to the place the guy had been standing when Violet saw him.

Two cigarette butts lay on the ground, proving he'd been there a while.

But why park his car and walk into the woods to smoke a cigarette?

Dev leaned a shoulder against the trunk of the old maple, imitating the position the guy had been in. Through a break in the trees, he could see a slender figure picking up toys in the yard.

I saw something interesting.

Dev's jaw clenched.

He'd seen Jenna.

Jenna tossed Logan's squirt gun into the plastic bin with a little more force than necessary.

What had just happened?

One minute "Marshal Dev" had been saving her cabin from a buffalo stampede, the next minute he'd looked as if he wanted to destroy her issue of *Twin City Trends.*

In the past, Jenna had had to deflect the occasional critical comment about the magazine from people who didn't understand its purpose, but Dev's reaction hadn't made sense.

She was surprised he'd even heard of the magazine, given the fact it targeted people living in an urban area.

Logan had disappeared in his room shortly after Dev left, the gentle click of the door as it closed somehow more heartbreaking than if he'd slammed it shut.

He didn't understand the reason for Dev's abrupt departure. And to be honest, neither did she.

"Aunt Jenna?" Tori's lilting voice drifted through the kitchen window. "Your phone is making a noise."

Jenna's breath caught in her throat. Was Shelly finally returning her call?

She dropped the paintbrushes into a bucket of soapy water and hurried back inside. The low hum of her BlackBerry guided her to the kitchen table. She snatched it up and read the name on the screen.

The missed call wasn't from Shelly, but from Marlene Sinclair, the executive editor at *Trends*.

Why was she calling on a Saturday...

Jenna yanked a chair away from the table and sagged into it.

Because the deadline for her weekly blog was Friday.

She'd *never* missed a deadline.

The steady thump of Jenna's heart began to pump in her ears like a bass drum as she dialed Marlene's number. Her boss wasn't the type of person who accepted excuses or apologies. She expected her staff to get things right the first time.

Something Jenna had never had a problem with until now.

"Hello." The brisk, businesslike tone scraped against Jenna's already raw nerves.

"Marlene? This is Jen—" She didn't get a chance to finish.

"Jenna, yes. It's good to hear from you."

It was?

"I saw that I missed your call and I'm—"

"Oh, don't worry about that." Marlene brushed the prequel to Jenna's apology aside. "I was calling to talk to you about your blog."

"I thought so. I'm not sure what happened…" Jenna bit her lip, knowing that wasn't totally true. She'd had every intention of writing her blog until Logan had turned up missing.

And Dev had invited them over for dinner.

"Have you checked the inbox today? It's flooded with letters from your readers."

Jenna expelled a slow breath. "Not yet. And I promise this won't happen again."

A chuckle penetrated the rushing sound in Jenna's ears. "I hope that isn't true. The readers are used to you being serious, but this piece revealed another side of you. It was fresh. Funny. Everyone loved it."

Everyone loved what? Jenna wanted to shout. There must have been some mistake. Maybe Marlene was referring to the column she'd written the week before.

"I have to admit that I had my reservations about you taking time off," Marlene continued. "But after I read your blog, I'm beginning to think you should stay in Mirror Lake a little longer."

"I didn't *post* a blog this week. I—" *Just say it, Jenna* "—missed my deadline."

"I know, but Dawn intervened on your behalf."

"Dawn?" Jenna choked out before she could stop herself.

Dawn Gallagher didn't intervene on anyone's behalf unless it worked to her advantage. And she'd resented Jenna from the moment Marlene had assigned her the City Girl column. She also had her eye on an upcoming promotion—the same one Jenna had been hoping for.

"I left her in charge while I toured Alex and Bernice Scott's theater camp for at-risk teens. It took months to get them to agree to an interview, you know.

"Anyway, Dawn forwarded the email you sent to me. She said everyone in the break room thought it was hysterical."

The only email Jenna remembered sending was a humorous story about Fred. The fish. She'd included it in the note she'd written to Marlene, thanking her for letting her take time off for a family emergency.

She hadn't meant for anyone else to read it.

"Listen, I've got another call coming in. We'll talk when you come in on Monday."

And there it was. The reality that Jenna had been trying to avoid.

"I don't think I'll be back in the office on Monday, Marlene. My sister isn't home yet." She hadn't shared the details about what had happened with Shelly, only that she needed to take care of her niece and nephew for a few days.

"Dawn offered to take over your weekly column if it's too much for you right now."

Of course she had.

Jenna could envision the catlike gleam in Dawn's eyes. Her coworker turned everything into a competition. It wouldn't have surprised Jenna to discover that Dawn had printed the story about Fred *hoping* that Jenna's readers would hate it. When that backfired, she oh-so-thoughtfully offered to take Jenna's place.

"That's not necessary, Marlene. I thought I would go through the archives and run some of the favorites again."

"I suppose I can give you a few more days…but only if you write another article like this one. Apparently your readers like 'fish out of water' stories. No pun intended." Marlene chuckled. "It's a perfect summer series. Our city girl in the wilderness. Catching fish and fighting gigantic spiders."

That's right. Jenna winced. She'd mentioned the spider, too.

"There must be some way you can tap into the quirks of a small town. Find some inspiration for another article."

Yes, there was.

And Jenna had a sinking feeling that her name was Gabby Bunker.

"We haven't received any other complaints of a person fitting that description."

"But you'll check into it, right?" Dev followed the harried young officer, who didn't appear old enough to own a razor let alone a handgun, as he strode across the parking lot to the squad car.

"I'll get to it. A hay wagon rolled over near the county line and they asked for our help to direct traffic."

Dev locked down his rising frustration. He'd cornered the officer as he was leaving the police department and told him about the trespasser on Jenna's property.

"Is there a problem, Trip?"

Dev hadn't heard anyone come up behind him. He half turned and found his character being measured by a guy who was either ex-military or a cop. Or both. Even in jeans and a paint-spattered T-shirt, the air of authority was unmistakable.

"Hey, Chief." The officer took advantage of the

interruption to dive into the driver's seat of the patrol car. "I'm on my way to a call but this guy wants to file a complaint. Someone trespassing on his property."

The window began to scroll up again before Dev could correct him.

"I'll take care of it."

"Thanks, Chief." The squad car peeled out of the parking lot, red and blue lights flashing.

The police chief himself.

Thank you, God.

Dev sent a silent prayer to the heavens for sending someone along who might actually take the situation seriously.

Dev had heard the city council had sworn in Jake Sutton, a former Milwaukee undercover drug officer, as police chief the previous year, but until now there'd never been an occasion to warrant a formal introduction. Until now.

Amber eyes swung back to him. Narrowed. "What can I do for you, McGuire?"

"Should I be nervous that you know my name?" Dev was only half joking.

Jake shrugged. "A person who works so hard not to get noticed gets noticed."

Dev would have to remember that.

"Come on inside." Jake fished a set of keys from the front pocket of his jeans. "No sense baking in the parking lot. My office is air-conditioned."

"It's Saturday. Aren't you off duty?"

"There's no such thing." It was a statement, not a complaint.

Dev followed him inside the brick building and down the narrow corridor. Jake's office was small, with a window overlooking the park. He motioned to a leather chair. "Grab a seat. The first coat of paint in my dining room is drying and I promised Emma I'd be back in half an hour. With ice cream. You don't break a promise like that."

A photograph of an adolescent boy with sandy blond hair and light blue eyes grinned at Dev from a frame made out of seashells and pieces of glass.

Jake caught him looking. "My son Jeremy. He's twelve."

The kid's bright smile reminded him of Logan. Guilt reared up, ready to go another round.

Dev regretted his abrupt departure, but if he hadn't left when he did, he might not have seen the guy lurking in the woods.

Jake sat down behind the desk and pushed a pile of paperwork aside. "Trip said someone was trespassing on your property?"

"Technically it was my neighbor's land, but I was the one who saw him."

"Your neighbor." Jake frowned. "Jenna Gardner?"

Something in the chief's expression set off

Dev's internal alarm. According to Jenna, she hadn't been in Mirror Lake for more than a week.

"Do you know her?"

The police chief made a noise left open to interpretation. "Why don't you give me the specifics?"

Dev gave Jake the details, along with a description of the man and the vehicle he'd been driving.

"It's too bad you couldn't get a plate number." Jake plucked a pen from a leather cylinder on the desk and scratched something on a piece of paper. "I'll tell my officers to keep an eye out for the vehicle or someone fitting that description."

Dev leaned forward. "That's it?"

The question surprised them both.

"He wasn't breaking any laws," Jake said after a moment.

"You think I'm overreacting," Dev said flatly.

"People from outside the area tend to think that if there aren't any 'no trespassing signs' posted every six feet, they can go wherever they please," Jake said. "The guy you met could have gotten out of his car to stretch his legs for a few minutes. Took a walk in the woods, just like he said."

It was a reasonable explanation. Except that Dev couldn't forget the smirk on the guy's face. The gleam in his eyes.

"I suppose you're right."

"You know Jenna well?" There was a speculative look in the chief's eyes now.

"I didn't say that." Why did Dev suddenly feel as if the tables had turned and he was the one under scrutiny? "But I do know she's living alone in that cabin with two small children and a guy who might have a rap sheet a mile long was hiding behind a tree, watching her."

"You *think* he was watching her. But I understand your concern and I'll ask the officer on night duty to drive past Jenna's cabin a few times."

"He won't see anything. The cabin is at the end of a long driveway." Dev tried not to let his frustration show. "Isn't there some kind of neighborhood watch program?"

"As a matter of fact there is. Would you like to sign up?"

"Me?"

Sutton smiled.

"You're her closest neighbor."

Chapter Eleven

"Violet's here!"

Logan dashed past Jenna on his way to the door.

The realization that she wanted to hug the dog rather than scold her was a sign that she needed to go back to the city.

"We'll take her—" Home.

The sentence died when Jenna saw not only the dog, but Dev, on the porch.

Tori lifted her arms and Dev scooped her up as if it were the most natural thing in the world. She looped her arms around his neck and pushed her face close to his, nose to nose.

"We. Missed. You."

Dev's eyes met hers over Tori's head and Jenna felt her traitorous heart kick in response.

"I thought you had plans for this evening." The words slipped out before she could prevent them.

"I do." Dev set Tori on the floor. "But I wouldn't mind some company. Interested in joining me?"

"Yes!"

Her niece and nephew answered the question before Jenna had a chance to speak.

"Jenna?" Dev looked at her.

Seriously? She was supposed to be the killjoy who wiped the smiles off those two adorable little faces?

"Where are we going?"

"To see a show." Dev smiled and set Tori down. "You'll need to wear jeans, a long-sleeved shirt and a jacket. And something practical on your feet. No heels."

"A formal dress code?" Jenna strove to keep her tone light, not wanting Dev to think that she'd been disappointed—or hurt—by his abrupt departure earlier that afternoon.

"And it will be strictly enforced."

"It sounds…interesting." She shouldn't have accepted.

"It sounds like fun!" Logan was already heading into the bedroom to change his clothes.

"I promise you won't regret it."

Didn't Dev realize that was the reason why she was hesitating? Jenna had believed promises before and lived to regret it. And now Dev was asking her to trust him.

"Think of it as a field trip," he added.

Which was the reason she had no choice but to go along. No matter how Dev felt about her, this outing was for Logan and Tori.

"We'll be right out."

Jenna helped Tori find her jacket and then quickly slipped on the pair of hiking shoes that had arrived with the shipment of new clothes she'd ordered for the children. She would probably never have an opportunity to wear them again, but they were similar to the pair she'd seen Abby wearing the day of the housewarming party.

Dev was waiting on the porch when Jenna shepherded the children outside a few minutes later. They took the path through the woods but when they got to Dev's cabin, he continued across the yard and led them to another trail that curved around the shoreline.

"Where are we going?" Tori whispered.

"You don't have to whisper," Logan told her.

"I know. But it feels like I should."

Jenna understood what Tori meant. The mournful call of a loon occasionally broke the silence as they followed Dev deeper into the woods. He shortened his stride to match Logan's, moving with the confidence of someone who'd done this a thousand times.

Every so often, Dev would stop to point things out. The shaggy silhouette of an owl perched on a branch. A fresh raccoon track in the sand. The wink of a firefly in the grass. The slap of a beaver's tail against the water, alerting its mate to their presence.

Sights and sounds Jenna would never have noticed if Dev wasn't with them.

They hiked up a small rise with only the narrow beam from Dev's flashlight and a sliver of moon to guide them. He stopped at the top and set his canvas backpack on the ground. "We're here."

Jenna looked around. All she saw were trees and…trees.

"Where—"

"Look up." Dev suddenly stood beside her, the heat from his body like a physical touch.

Jenna tipped her head back and felt the breath tangle in her lungs.

A black velvet ceiling stretched above them, the stars close enough to touch. Flawless as diamonds and each one just as stunning in its clarity.

"Everyone have a seat." Dev's lips moved upward in a smile. "The show is about to start."

Jenna felt a shimmer of anticipation. Dev McGuire had some very unusual ideas about the best way to spend an evening.

Violet, who seemed to understand the proper protocol, waited for Dev to spread a blanket out on the dew-tipped grass.

Logan and Tori flopped down immediately, burrowing into the fleece blanket Dev pulled from his backpack. Jenna settled beside them and rested her chin on her knees, a feeling of peace spreading over her that she couldn't explain.

In the city, artificial light muted the beauty of the night sky. Jenna couldn't remember the last time she'd even noticed it. On the nights she worked late, she walked to her car on autopilot, focused on planning her agenda for the next day.

Tori snuggled against her as Dev dropped to one knee and wrestled another object from his backpack.

"Sweet." Logan wiggled closer to get a better look and aimed the flashlight beam at the telescope Jenna had noticed propped in the corner of Dev's living room.

"Do you want to help me set it up?"

"Sure!" Jenna found herself holding the flashlight as Logan dropped to his knees beside Dev and traced his fingers over the letters written on the side of the telescope.

"Who's Jason?" he asked.

Dev almost dropped the telescope, a knee-jerk reaction to hearing his brother's name.

His parents never talked about Jason. Brent McGuire buried his grief as deep as the footings of the structures he built. His mother wore hers like a mourning cloak, a silent but public display for everyone to see.

Only Talia talked about Jason. She called Dev

on his birthday. Repeated his favorite sayings and remembered his dreams.

"My brother." Dev pushed the words out, aware that Jenna was listening.

"Did he give it to you?"

All Dev could do was nod as a memory crashed over him.

Jason had asked for a telescope for his twelfth birthday and surprisingly enough, their parents had granted the request. He'd become obsessed with mapping the stars and could name every one of the constellations.

Dev could still remember the night he'd come home from a date and Jason had met him at the door, barely able to contain his excitement.

"Come outside, Dev. I have to show you something."

"Let me guess—you found a new galaxy that no scientist has ever seen before."

"No."

"You struck oil in the backyard."

"Better."

Dev had followed him onto the spacious deck of their home more out of resignation than curiosity. Jason's telescope was aimed at the stars. Nothing unusual about that.

"So what did you discover?"

"Do you believe in God, Dev?"

"Why?" Dev had chosen the safest response.

"Because when I was looking at the Andromeda Galaxy tonight, I saw him."

"You saw God? I think you need to cut back on the Mountain Dew and get more sleep."

Jason's smile hadn't dimmed. *"Okay, maybe I didn't actually see him, but I realized he has to be real. The universe is so amazing. So big...something has to be...bigger."*

Dev had laughed. *Laughed.*

Even now, twenty years later, the memory churned a sick feeling in his gut.

"Don't tell Mom and Dad or they'll take that thing away from you."

Of course his kid brother hadn't taken his advice. Jason decided to share his newfound faith over brunch at the country club the following Sunday. To make matters worse, he'd added another stunning revelation.

He'd informed their father that he wasn't going to join the family company. He wanted to build houses for poor people instead of condominiums and golf courses for the wealthy.

Their mother had knocked over her wineglass. Red liquid had bled onto the Battenberg lace tablecloth while all the color had bled out of Brent McGuire's face.

The telescope disappeared the next day.

Dev had stumbled upon it several years later, propped in the corner of their grandfather's cabin.

One night, he had actually worked up the courage to set it up on the deck.

The night he'd realized Jason was right.

"Dev?"

He jerked out of his reverie at the tentative touch of Jenna's hand on his arm.

His heart shifted into second gear and he eased away from her.

"Sorry."

Maybe this hadn't been such a great idea. But as hard as he tried, he hadn't been able to shake the thought of the guy in black skulking through the trees.

He'd taken Jake Sutton's suggestion to heart and decided that keeping an eye on Jenna and the kids was his civic duty. The only way to do that without looking like the stalker in the woods that he was concerned about was to invite them on a field trip.

For a few hours, he could set aside his disgust that Jenna worked for *Twin City Trends*. Especially when those big blue eyes brimmed with concern for *him*.

Dev didn't deserve her comfort or understanding.

He blew out a slow breath, aware that he'd taken too long to answer Logan's innocent question.

"Jason is my brother." Dev carefully tucked the memory aside and worked up a smile. "Now, who wants to get a close up look at the Milky Way?"

Jenna recognized a diversionary tactic when she saw one.

The shadows hadn't concealed the change in his expression when Logan asked him about the name etched on the side of the telescope.

She tried to remember if Dev had mentioned having a brother. Was there some kind of rivalry going on? Had they had a falling out? Because something had triggered that strong response. Something he didn't want to talk about.

"Tori can go first." Logan nudged his sister forward.

Dev gave him a solemn wink of approval, aware of the sacrifice that had just been made. He knelt down and positioned the telescope for a petite five-year-old.

While Logan and Tori absorbed every word, Jenna's attention shifted from the stunning night sky to the man patiently pointing out Orion and Aquila, the Eagle.

"What do you say we let your aunt have a turn now?"

"Me?" Jenna snapped back to attention.

"You have to. It's awesome, Aunt Jenna!" Logan moved out of the way, leaving Jenna with no choice but to take part or be labeled a party pooper.

As she knelt down, Jenna felt the feather-soft brush of Dev's hand and the responding shiver of awareness. He went so still that Jenna wondered if Dev had felt it, too.

"Cold?"

"Yes." Although just the opposite was true, Jenna thought with rising panic.

Dev took her words at face value because the next moment, he'd stripped off his butter soft chambray shirt and draped it over her shoulders.

"Thanks." The word sounded more like the croak of a frog.

"The temperature is starting to drop at night. In a few weeks, the trees are going to start to change color."

And she would be long gone by then, watching the trees change color from her office window.

Tori rubbed her eyes and curled up next to Violet on the blanket. "I want to see—" She yawned. "—a shooting star."

"I'm afraid I can't show you one of those." Dev chuckled. "Shooting stars are flashy but they're a bit unpredictable. You might get lucky and see one, but a moment later, it's gone." He sat down on the blanket and Tori immediately nestled into the curve of his arm. "How about I show you my favorite star instead?"

"Okay."

Logan dropped down beside them and curled an arm around Violet, too.

"Do you see those five stars?"

Logan bobbed his head. "That's the Big Dipper."

"You're right. Now follow a line to…there." There was absolute silence as the children tracked the movement of Dev's finger to another star winking above them. "That one is Polaris. The North Star."

"It's not very bright." Tori sounded a wee bit disappointed.

"That's true, but it's still pretty special." Dev leaned back, settling his weight on his elbows as he tipped his face to the sky. "Sailors and explorers looked to the North Star to help them remain on course.

"It might not be as flashy or get attention like a shooting star, but it's the one you can trust to always be there. To help you keep moving in the right direction."

A constant.

Something that didn't change from day to day like fashion trends or the stock market or opinion polls.

"Kate said that God does that," Logan said.

"She's right." Dev smiled down at him. "Sometimes I think that God put the North Star there so we would remember."

Jenna couldn't look at Dev as the words settled deep, shifting her beliefs and values to make room for…for what? Another nice thought? Or truth.

"I like this place." Tori's eyelids fluttered. "Can we sleep here tonight?"

The question instantly propelled Dev and Jenna to their feet.

"I think we better be heading back." Before she finished the sentence, Dev was already packing up his gear.

They followed the path to the cabin in silence. Dev carrying Tori in his arms, Jenna holding tight to Logan's small hand and Violet padding alongside them.

She shoved a hand in her pocket and fumbled for the key as they climbed the steps to the porch. Jenna wasn't sure if she could blame the sudden trembling in her fingers on Logan's grip or her close proximity to Dev.

She opened her mouth to say goodbye when he took the key, unlocked the door and walked inside.

"I'll take care of Logan while you get Tori ready for bed."

Jenna was too tired from battling her own emotions to argue.

Dev flipped on the light and everyone trooped inside. Jenna guided Tori to the bedroom and folded the comforter back. She'd already decided to replace the worn bedding before Shelly returned, something that would coordinate with the pink walls.

On the other side of the door, Jenna could hear

Logan chattering on about the constellations, his voice an excited soprano against the low rumble of Dev's bass.

By the time she finished combing the tangles from Tori's hair and returned to the living room, Logan and Dev were on the floor, picking up pieces of the frontier town and putting them back in a plastic storage crate.

It brought back memories of a saucy wink and teasing smile.

And the way Dev had reacted when she'd told him that she worked for *Twin City Trends*.

"Time for bed now." Time to put some distance between her and Dev.

"'Night." Tori pulled on Dev's hand until they were eye to eye. "Guess what?"

"What?"

"The North Star's my fav'rite, too."

"Sweet dreams, sunshine."

"I will." Tori flitted toward the bedroom.

"Thank you for inviting us along." Jenna put on a polite smile. "It was very…educational."

Dev's elusive smile surfaced. "Didn't I promise you'd enjoy it?"

That was the problem. Jenna had enjoyed it. Too much.

And she wasn't used to people keeping their promises.

Chapter Twelve

"Jenna! Over here!"

Kate's smiling face was the first one Jenna saw when she walked through the doors of Church of the Pines the next morning. Standing beside her, one arm wrapped around her slim waist, was a man who could have easily made the cover of *Twin City Trends*.

"Alex!" Logan and Tori had no qualms about rushing to his side.

Alex Porter's cool, jade green eyes instantly warmed a few degrees as he bent down to hug them.

Tori wriggled free, forehead pleated in a frown as she carefully looked him over, small hands planted on her hips.

"You're all better!" she announced.

"I sure am." Alex winked at her. "No more spots."

"Do you like my new dress?" Tori clasped a

handful of the yellow ruffle circling the hem and twirled around. "Aunt Jenna bought it for me. Pink is my favorite color but yellow is my second favorite."

"It's beautiful," Alex said promptly. "You look like a daisy."

Judging from the smile on Tori's face, he couldn't have paid the little girl a greater compliment.

Jenna watched the exchange in bemusement. She could hold her own in different social situations—it came with her job—but even she had been a little intimidated by Alex Porter. In Chicago, he and Abby had moved through the upper levels of the social stratosphere like royalty.

The family's small chain of luxury hotels were well known throughout the Midwest. Porter Lakeside had even been featured in the travel section of *Twin City Trends* the previous year.

Jenna had met with Alex briefly following his release from the hospital to thank him for coming to the children's rescue.

Alex had listened, polite but aloof, and then proceeded to question Jenna about her plans. Was she going to stay in Mirror Lake? Take the children back to Minnesota? Whatever Jenna had said must have satisfied Alex because she'd been allowed to leave.

Kate had pulled her aside later and explained that Alex had become rather attached to Logan and Tori while they were staying with her. What she'd witnessed was the man's unique— Jenna was sure Kate had added the word "highhanded" below her breath—way of expressing concern.

"Good morning, Alex." Jenna resisted the urge to fidget when that pair of jade eyes zeroed in on her.

"Jenna. It's nice to see you again." His manner had thawed considerably since the last time they'd met.

"We're so glad you came this morning." Kate pulled Jenna in for a hug. "There's a picnic after the service this morning. I hope you and the kids will be able to stay for awhile."

Jenna hesitated. She hadn't planned to attend church but Tori had bounced on her bed, awake before the birds and already dressed in one of the outfits Jenna had had shipped from one of her favorite boutiques.

"We have to go to church, Aunt Jenna," she'd informed her. "Kate says that God likes to see his children together."

Church attendance had never been encouraged in Jenna's family. Once, when Jenna was about Logan's age, a teenage girl had knocked on the door and handed her a flyer advertising a week-long vacation Bible school being held at the church she attended.

Jenna had taken it to her mother, excited at the

possibility of attending, but Nola had barely given it a cursory glance before tossing it in the waste-basket.

"No sense keeping it," her mother had said. "We'll be gone by then."

And that had been the end of it.

"I'm not sure about the picnic." Jenna searched for a reasonable excuse. "I didn't bring a dish to pass—"

Kate waved aside Jenna's protest. "There's always plenty of food."

"Kate and Abby singlehandedly make sure of it," Alex murmured.

"Abby bakes to relax," Kate explained. "Alex arrived yesterday and we now have three dozen muffins, two pans of cinnamon rolls and a lemon Bundt cake. I won't comment on any correlation between the two."

Instead of appearing offended by her teasing, Alex grinned. "All I told Abby was that I planned to move here before Christmas."

"Exactly."

The couple smiled at each other and Jenna felt a twinge of envy.

She wouldn't have thought that Kate, a woman who'd never ventured beyond the border of her home state would have anything in common with a high-powered executive like Alex Porter, and yet it was clear the two were deeply in love. Abby had mentioned that her brother planned to make Mirror Lake his permanent home.

A few weeks ago, she would have thought he was crazy. But now…Jenna pulled her thoughts in line.

Not going there.

Music drifted through the foyer. Through the narrow windows in the doors of the sanctuary, Jenna could see Zoey at the piano.

Kate chuckled. "There's our cue."

Logan took Jenna by the hand. "I'll show you where we sit."

Several people smiled at them and greeted the children by name as they made their way down the center aisle. To Jenna's surprise, some of them greeted her by name, too. The woman who had waved to them on Main Street used her pink cane to brake next to the pew. She peered down at Jenna.

"Delia Peake," she bellowed, thrusting out a hand.

"Jenna. Jenna Gardner."

"I know who you are." The rubber tip on the end of the cane thumped the floor. "Saw your name on the list of new members a few days ago."

"What—" Jenna didn't have time to finish the sentence.

"I'll see you at our next meeting." Delia dipped into a purse that had gone out of style twenty years ago, handed Logan and Tori some Hershey's Kisses and continued down the aisle.

Jenna felt a light tap on her shoulder and turned to see the Sutton family sitting behind them.

"Don't worry," Emma whispered. "Delia has that effect on everyone."

"Do you know what she's talking about?" Jenna whispered back. "I didn't sign up for anything."

"Unfortunately, that's never been a prerequisite around here." Jake interjected with a wry smile that softened the line of his jaw and made him seem more approachable.

"Ask Kate." Emma handed a hymnal to Jeremy. "She might know."

"Know?" Jake echoed. "She's probably the one who put Jenna's name on the list."

Emma batted her husband's arm. "Be nice."

The prelude ended and the pastor strode up the narrow aisle, pausing to greet people along the way.

Matthew and Zoey exchanged a smile as he approached the pulpit, and Jenna saw several of the older women nod in approval. The congregation had obviously given the couple its blessing.

Bypassing the simple oak podium, Matt came to stand in front of the congregation.

With a smile as easygoing as his attire, khaki pants and a white dress shirt with the sleeves rolled back to reveal his muscular forearms, the man didn't fit Jenna's mental image of a pastor. The first time they'd met was in the small chapel of the hospital, when Jenna had brought the children to visit Alex.

Matt had joined hands with Kate and Zoey in prayer, the three of them linked together by friendship and their shared faith.

Jenna had waited in the doorway, once again feeling as if she were on the outside looking in.

She didn't understand why it seemed so easy for them to put their trust in something they couldn't see. Even Tori and Logan said bedtime prayers, their simple faith stirring emotions in Jenna that had been dormant for years.

Tori snuggled against Jenna's side. If it weren't for her niece and nephew, she wouldn't be sitting in church this morning.

"God wants us to come to him with the faith of a child," Caitlin had told her once.

Maybe that was part of the problem. From an early age, Jenna had been in charge of the family. Taken care of Shelly and their mother. Managed the household and the secrets.

If you're here, God, if you're listening...could you let me know?

The simple prayer rose out of her heart and took wing on its own volition, born from a need that Jenna hadn't known existed until now. She looked around almost guiltily, afraid for a moment that she'd spoken the words out loud. But everyone was looking at Matt as he leafed through the pages of a worn leather Bible.

"The heavens declare the glory of the Lord. The skies proclaim the work of his hands. Day after day they pour forth speech. Night after night they display knowledge.

There is no speech or language where their voice is not heard. Their voice goes out into all the earth. Their words to the ends of the world."

"This is our call to worship this morning." Matt's smile swept over the congregation, as warm as the sunlight streaming through the stained glass windows. "Let's pray."

Everyone bowed their head, but Jenna didn't hear what Matt was saying. Everything around her disappeared.

All Jenna saw was night sky stretched over her head. And the faint glow of Polaris, Dev's favorite star.

"It's the one you can trust to always be there, to help you keep moving in the right direction."

Jenna's breath knotted in her lungs as the verse unfolded in her heart.

The heavens declare the glory of God.

As unbelievable as it seemed, God had just answered her prayer.

* * *

Dev swiped at the beads of sweat collecting on his brow with the back of his hand. He'd spent the better part of the afternoon scraping the old finish off his grandfather's canoe, a project that had slowly worked its way up his summer to do list.

The project kept his hands busy but unfortunately, his thoughts kept straying to the woman who lived next door. It was becoming a habit.

Violet streaked past him and Dev caught a glimpse of something dangling from her mouth.

"Hey, you. Get back here."

Of course she didn't listen.

Dev wiped his hands off on a rag and followed Violet to the willow that bowed over the shoreline, her favorite place to hide contraband.

Violet, crouched over whatever treasure she'd found, gave him a bright "hey, Dev, what's happening" smile as he swept the boughs aside.

"Okay, what did you find—" Dev bit back a groan when he saw the coonskin cap between her paws.

Somehow, his lug of a dog had managed to steal Logan's favorite hat. Leaving him no choice but to return it. It was as if Violet and Logan had worked out a plan to keep him and Jenna together.

"You did this on purpose, didn't you?" Dev picked up the hat to assess the damage. Wet tail.

No holes. "You didn't see your buddy all day, so you figured out a way to invite yourself over."

Violet barked at him. A "right back at you" bark, reminding Dev that he was the one who'd taken Jenna and the kids on a field trip to watch the stars the night before.

"That was different," Dev muttered. "Sutton deputized me. It's not like I had a choice. Someone had to make sure that guy didn't come back."

Violet rolled to her feet and flipped her tail as she trotted past. The canine equivalent of "talk to the hand."

If Talia saw him now, arguing with his four-legged roommate, she'd stage an intervention.

Dev glanced at the setting sun, wondering if he should wait until the following morning to return the hat. But knowing how important it was to Logan, he decided to leave it on the porch for Jenna to find.

Then turn tail and run home like the coward you are.

He wasn't running away from Jenna. He was giving her what she wanted. Space. She was the one who'd drawn the line in the sand. Was it his fault that Violet and Logan pretended as if it didn't exist?

Great. Now he was arguing with his conscience.

Halfway to Jenna's cabin, Violet veered off course and forged a new path through the woods.

Dev didn't bother to whistle. If the dog was following a scent trail, he'd have more success if he followed *her*.

He found Violet planted at the base of a gnarled oak, fifty yards off the path. Looking up at the branches.

"Leave it alone, Violet." She might not have cornered a skunk this time but the chances that she'd sent a porcupine lumbering up the tree for cover were high enough to send Dev swiftly to her side.

"Let's go before you get someone riled up." As he took hold of her collar, he heard rustling in the leaves.

Dev glanced up, expecting to see a raccoon or a disgruntled porcupine clinging to the trunk of the tree.

What he saw was a small tennis shoe dangling above his head.

Chapter Thirteen

"Logan?"

Dev's heart slammed into his chest wall. He'd climbed a few trees back in the day, but the boy was a lot higher off the ground than he should have been. "What are you doing up there, buddy?"

The foot disappeared.

Violet looked at Dev and whined.

Dev looked around but there was no sign of Jenna and Tori. And it was clear that Logan didn't want to be found.

"Guess what Violet found." Dev held up the coonskin cap. "I'll bet you were wondering what happened to it."

"She can have it." Logan's voice drifted down. "I don't want it anymore."

Not good. Dev released a slow breath.

"Did something happen today?"

"I just don't want the hat anymore." Logan's voice stretched thin. "I can't be a real explorer anyway."

There was a truckload of hurt in the statement. "Do you want to talk about it?"

"N-no."

"Are you sure?"

"You can't do anything." Logan sounded so dejected—and so certain—that Dev took the statement as a personal challenge.

Maybe he couldn't solve the problem weighing those little shoulders down, but he could let Logan know there were people who cared enough to listen.

Dev reached for the lowest branch.

"Don't move. I'm coming up."

Tori dove under the covers the moment Jenna peeked in the bedroom to check on her.

"Did you brush your teeth?"

The lump underneath the blankets moved. "Yes."

"Wash your face and hands?"

"Uh-huh," came the muffled response. "'Night, Aunt Jenna."

Jenna lingered in the doorway. This felt too easy. Tori's bedtime ritual included reading a chapter out of *The Secret Garden* and arranging an intricate barricade of stuffed animals around the pillow.

"Is everything okay?"

"I'm sleepy." An exaggerated yawn followed the statement. "Can you turn out the light?"

Tori. Asking her to turn out the light. Jenna didn't need a parenting book to figure out that something strange was going on.

She made her way over to the side of the bed. "Don't I get a good night hug?"

"Okay." The blanket dropped an inch. With her wisps of blond hair sticking straight up and those wide blue eyes, Tori resembled a baby owl.

"If I remember correctly, a hug involves *arms*," Jenna teased, tugging on the corner of the blanket.

Tori yanked it back up, but not before Jenna caught a glimpse of yellow eyelet trim. Now she understood. Tori hadn't changed into her pajamas yet.

"Why didn't you change your clothes, sweetie? You don't want to wear your pretty new dress to bed."

Tori's lower lip slid forward. "Yes, I do."

Jenna stared down at her in astonishment. What was going on with her niece and nephew? They'd been acting strangely all afternoon.

She'd noticed a subtle change in their mood after the church service that morning. The children in the congregation had been dismissed for children's church midway through the service, leaving Jenna with Kate and the Suttons.

After the service, when everyone made a beeline for the tables laden with food in a grassy area near the parking lot, Logan had balked when Jenna began to move in that direction.

"Can we go home now?"

"Don't you want to stay for the picnic?" Jenna had asked, shocked that Logan didn't want to spend a little more time with his friend Jeremy.

He'd scraped a trench in the gravel with the tip of his shoe and refused to meet her eyes. "I don't feel like it."

Jenna had turned to her niece. "Tori?"

The siblings exchanged a silent look that Jenna had been unable to interpret. Then Tori had folded her hands over her stomach.

"I think my tummy hurts."

That settled the matter. Jenna loaded them into the car and drove to the cabin. Logan went straight inside, not even pausing to see if Violet was lurking nearby.

As the afternoon wore on, he hadn't expressed any interest in playing outside and responded in monosyllables whenever Jenna tried to start a conversation.

When both the children had refused to eat supper, her concern increased. Tori had requested a bath earlier than usual so Jenna had left Logan playing in the living room while she washed Tori's hair. Now Jenna understood why she'd dashed into the bedroom and closed the door.

"Dresses are for daytime and pajamas are for night," Jenna said gently.

"I don't want to wear pajamas."

Tori's eyes darkened with panic, not rebellion, telling Jenna this wasn't an act of defiance. She sat down on the edge of the mattress.

"Why not?" she asked simply.

Tori wrapped the blanket more tightly around herself. "I don't want my dress to get lost."

"It won't get lost. I'll hang it up in the closet and it will be right there when you wake up in the morning."

"But—" A tear rolled down Tori's cheek. "—what if we have to leave and you forget to bring it?"

Jenna suddenly understood the reason for the fear she saw in her niece's eyes. Things had been left behind before. Forgotten.

Jenna wished she didn't remember what that felt like.

God, what do I say?

The prayer slipped out before Jenna could stop it. She had no idea how to reassure a little girl who had been forced to abandon her things in the middle of the night. Who never knew when her mother would decide to pick up and move again.

"I'll tell you what," she said quietly. "You put your pajamas on and then we can fold up your dress and put it right next to your pillow."

Tori glanced at her stuffed dog. "Can Princess sleep next to it? It's her favorite dress, too."

Jenna nodded, not trusting herself to speak. While Tori changed into her nightgown, she shook out the wrinkles in the dress and carefully arranged it next to Tori's pillow.

"How is this?"

"Good." Tori's finger drifted over the eyelet collar. "Yellow is my new favorite color."

"It's mine, too."

Tori grinned and tucked Princess in the crook of her arm. "'Night, Aunt Jenna."

Jenna reached down and brushed a wisp of hair from Tori's cheek. "I'll see you in the morning."

Blue eyes searched Jenna's. "Promise?"

"I promise."

Satisfied, Tori burrowed deeper under the quilt and closed her eyes.

Jenna backed out of the bedroom and closed the door halfway.

"Logan?"

The frontier town was gone, packed away in the plastic storage bin.

And there was no sign of her nephew.

Not tonight, Logan, she pleaded silently. She wasn't sure she could face Dev right now. The situation with Tori had left her feeling raw. Exposed. The man had an uncanny way of searching for things below the surface. Things Jenna had always kept hidden.

Ten years ago, she'd put a painful past behind her. Now she was reliving it through the eyes of her five-year-old niece. Frequent moves. Constant change. Broken promises.

Would Tori eventually become jaded? Slow to trust? And what could she say that would make a difference in the little girl's life? Jenna hadn't been able to help Shelly.

She walked around the back of the cabin, swatting at the mosquitoes that rose from the grass.

A cool breeze winnowed through the trees and a bank of ominous looking clouds had crowded along the horizon.

"Logan?" Jenna scanned the woods, searching for a glimpse of the red shirt Logan had changed into after church. "It's time to come inside and take your bath now."

A branch snapped a few yards off the path and relief washed through her. Maybe he hadn't sneaked off to see Violet after all.

"Logan?" Jenna waded through an ankle-deep carpet of emerald ferns. "Is that you? Can you hear me?"

Branches snapped in quick succession, as if something very large—larger than Logan—was making its way toward her.

Jenna grabbed the closest stick she could find. Just in case.

A blur of gray-and-brown fur and Violet appeared, tail wagging. Jenna had to admit the dog was a welcome sight because it meant her nephew was somewhere nearby.

Violet eyed the stick in her hand hopefully.

"Not right now." Jenna reached out to ruffle a velvety ear. "I'm looking for Logan."

"I'm up here."

Up here?

Jenna looked up and saw a small pair of feet dangling above her head. Way above her head.

Tiny spots began to dance in front of her eyes. Logan had to be at least fifteen feet off the ground.

"Are you stuck? Can you climb back down?" Jenna was already scoping out the branches, looking for the quickest way to reach her nephew and bring him to safety.

"Dev can help me."

"Dev isn't here, sweetie—"

"Ah…" The leaves rustled and a familiar face appeared. "As a matter of fact, he is."

"What are you two *doing* up there?" Jenna demanded.

Dev supposed it was a reasonable enough question. He just wished he could give Jenna a reasonable answer.

"We were talking," Logan said.

"Talking." Jenna repeated the word as if she'd never heard it before.

"Uh-huh. Dev said it's okay, 'cause sometimes you can find your words easier when you're sitting in a tree."

Accusing blue eyes met his and Dev braced himself for the repercussions, even while he silently acknowledged that reaching the safety of the ground wouldn't be the end of it. He'd talked to Logan—and now he had to talk to Jenna.

"I'm coming down first." Dev grabbed a handhold on the nearest branch. "Watch what I do, Logan, and you'll be fine. Don't look down." He heard a small chirp of distress from the audience of one on the ground. "Jenna?"

"What?"

"Don't look up."

Dev took it slow, giving Logan time to watch where he put his hands. His feet. Coming down was always a little more frightening, a little more difficult, than going up.

He swung to the ground and immediately turned his attention to Logan. "You're doing great. Keep it up."

Logan braced a hand against the trunk of the tree and anchored a foot against a branch. His foot slipped against the trunk of the tree and flecks of bark sifted down.

Jenna looked up.

"Logan!"

He'd *told* her not to look up.

"It's okay," Logan gasped, his forehead knit with concentration. "I watched Dev do it."

Jenna's eyes narrowed on him. Maybe that wasn't such a comforting reminder.

As Logan reached the last branch, Dev held up his arms. Without hesitation, the boy let go and dropped into them.

Jenna still looked a little pale when his feet touched the ground.

"Logan." Jenna's lips barely moved. "Let's go back to the cabin and I'll make some popcorn while you wash up. It's been a long day."

And it was about to get longer, Dev thought.

"Okay. Bye, Dev." Logan hugged Violet and shuffled away.

"Hey, buddy."

Logan glanced over his shoulder.

Dev held up the coonskin cap. "Aren't you forgetting something?"

A ghost of a smile touched the boy's lips. "I guess so."

Dev planted it on his head, straightened the damp tail. "It looks better on you than it does on Violet."

The smile grew. "Thanks."

Jenna opened her mouth to say something. Closed it again. Pivoted and walked away from him. Probably because at some point, she'd been told that if she couldn't say anything nice, don't say anything at all.

For a split second, Dev was tempted to let her go. Give her time to cool down. Then he remembered the brave front Logan had tried to put on—and the red-rimmed eyes he hadn't been able to hide.

"Jenna?"

She froze.

"Do you have a few minutes? I'd like to talk to you."

Jenna's pointed gaze bounced from him to the tree Logan had climbed.

Dev winced. "Both feet on the ground. Promise."

"I shouldn't." She flicked a look at the cabin. "Logan…"

"Actually, Logan is the reason I wanted to talk to you," Dev admitted. "I'll make it quick."

Jenna nodded once but didn't look at him as they fell in step together. She looked frustrated. And beautiful. The breeze toyed with the strands of silver hair that had escaped from a loose coil at the nape of her neck and Dev resisted the urge to tuck it back in place.

His hands curled inside his pockets instead.

"Inside? On the porch?" Jenna's clipped tone

warned Dev to make up his mind quickly so they could get this over with.

"Follow me." Dev headed toward an outcropping of rock on the shoreline. He didn't want Logan to overhear their conversation, but he knew Jenna wanted to be in clear sight of the cabin if one of the children needed her.

Violet quickly lost interest in them and went to look for crayfish hiding in the reeds.

"I can't believe you actually told a seven-year-old boy that it's easier to talk in a *tree*."

Dev had been trying to think of the best way to start when Jenna fired the first shot.

"Jenna—"

But she'd already reloaded, cutting him off. "And you know that I've asked Logan not to leave the yard without permission."

"I didn't encourage Logan to climb that tree." Dev drove a hand through his hair, reliving the moment he'd looked up and spotted the boy's feet above his head. It had sheered a decade from his life. "Violet was the one who discovered Logan in the tree. He'd climbed up there all by himself. I only went up after him because I was afraid he might fall."

Jenna's indignation drained away. "Logan disappeared while Tori and I were…while I was getting her ready for bed. I was afraid he might have run away again."

"Again?"

Jenna's lips tightened and she looked away.

"Logan didn't run away. He said he needed a quiet place to think."

"I'm sorry. I shouldn't have jumped to conclusions. I know you wouldn't put Logan in danger." Jenna sighed. "But something has been bothering Logan all day and he won't tell me what it is."

Dev took a deep breath. Prayed for guidance and wisdom.

"He told me."

Chapter Fourteen

"Why would he tell you?"

Jenna's eyes darkened in confusion.

Dev didn't take offense. He wasn't quite sure why Logan had confided in him, either. Not that it hadn't taken a little coaxing on his part.

"Sometimes it's easier to talk man-to-man."

Jenna's ragged sigh sliced through him. "Can you tell me what you talked about?"

"No." Dev didn't want to betray Logan's trust. "But I can talk about the canoe trip next weekend."

"Canoe trip." Jenna frowned and Dev could practically see the wheels turning. "I remember hearing Emma and Abby mention something about that after church this morning. The mentoring ministry is sponsoring the outing and both their husbands are planning to help."

"One of the adult volunteers gave Logan an invitation," Dev said.

"I didn't see it."

Dev retrieved a wrinkled square of florescent green paper from his pocket and handed it to her. He'd already read the contents. The daylong outing started at Abby's bed-and-breakfast and ended with an evening cookout.

The paper trembled as Jenna skimmed the contents. "He can't go."

"Why not?"

"Because Logan and Tori might not be here next week." Jenna handed the flyer back to him. "And I won't make Logan a promise that I can't keep."

"But your sister wouldn't leave immediately, would she?" Dev knew he was treading on dangerous ground, but he owed it to Logan to intervene. "If she's been in the hospital, wouldn't her doctor recommend some time at home to recover?"

Jenna knotted the tails of her shirt together in her lap. "I'm not sure. If Shelly doesn't get…better…soon, I'll have to take the children back to Minneapolis with me."

Dev didn't know why that information twisted his stomach in a knot. Jenna had made no secret of the fact that she couldn't wait to get back to the city.

"But what if they *are* here?" Dev knew how important the outing was to Logan. The boy had been in tears when he'd explained how much he wanted to go on the canoe trip. "Couldn't your sister make the arrangements—"

"No." Jenna jumped to her feet, poised for flight, but Dev caught hold of her hand.

"I don't understand."

"That's the problem."

Dev added an extra prayer for patience. "Then help me. I care about Logan."

And—*help me, Lord*—he was starting to care about Jenna, too.

Jenna glared up at him.

"Why are you pushing this?" she snapped. She tried to pull her hand away but Dev wouldn't let go.

"Because the canoe trip is important to Logan. He said that he's never been on one before."

The reminder that she'd failed her nephew scraped against Jenna's conscience. She should have tried harder to trace Shelly's whereabouts after Logan was born. If she had, maybe things would have been different.

"Shelly—" Jenna's throat closed, her control hanging on by a thread. What could she say about the sister she hadn't seen or heard from in seven years? "She might not be staying in Mirror Lake, either."

"But you don't know that for sure." Frustration sizzled in Dev's tone. "You might not like small towns, but your sister might want to make her home here. She could change her mind."

"She won't." Jenna knew that and so did the children. That's why Tori had worn her new dress to bed. She was afraid it would get left behind. Logan was upset because he had no idea where he would be living in a week.

"Shelly doesn't know how to stay in one place." Neither had their mother. Nola had been restless, always searching for something that she never found in the next town. After their father filed for divorce, it had gotten worse. And so had Nola's drinking problem. "Logan would be devastated if I gave him permission to go and then something happened."

"Maybe you could plan a substitute activity. Something Logan can look forward to. What else does he like to do?"

"I don't know." The words slipped out before Jenna could stop them. She was dimly aware that Dev hadn't let go of her hand. "I haven't seen Logan for seven years. *Seven years.* All I know is that he likes dogs and fishing and campfires."

And if it hadn't been for Dev, Jenna wouldn't have known that.

"I saw Logan once, right after he was born. And then Shelly, my sister...she left. I didn't even know Tori existed until Grace Eversea called last week."

It was as if a dam had burst inside of her. The

words kept coming, spilling over with her own fears and frustrations…

"They need so much and I don't even know where to start. Tori has nightmares. Logan carries the weight of the world on his shoulders. I have no idea what I'm doing. And Shelly—" She couldn't even say the words.

"She's in rehab, isn't she?" Dev asked softly.

Jenna's chin shot up. "How did you know that?"

"Conversations involving social workers and foster care, a mother who was in the hospital and no mention of a father. I put the pieces together."

Jenna couldn't look at him now. "You were right when you said they've been through a lot."

Dev's other hand reached up to cup her jaw. He tipped her chin until Jenna had no choice but to meet his eyes. The compassion she saw in them threatened to snip the last thread of her self-control.

"So have you."

Dev's hands closed over Jenna's shoulders and he drew her into his arms. For a moment, Jenna rested her forehead against the broad chest, inhaled a scent more potent than a designer cologne. Welcomed the slow, steady beat of his heart.

"You're doing a great job with Logan and Tori," Dev murmured. "You couldn't prevent the choices their mother made."

"I should have been there for her."

"You're with the kids now. And you're doing a great job."

Jenna wished she could believe him.

"You don't have to do this alone."

Yes, she did. She always had.

A fishing boat glided past the dock. The friendly whoops and hollers from the people waving at them from the bow brought Jenna back to her senses.

"I'm sorry." She forced herself to step away, when all she wanted to do was stay in Dev's arms. Safe. Secure.

"Jenna—" He reached for her hand but this time Jenna scooted out of reach.

"I have to check on the kids."

Jenna was equally relieved and disappointed when Dev didn't follow.

She'd blamed Shelly for running away.

Now who was guilty of doing the same thing?

In a neighborhood where ranch-style homes lined both sides of the street, Gabby Bunker lived in a tiny bungalow that looked like something straight off the pages of a fairy tale. Peach hollyhocks with delicate bell skirts swayed against the foundation. Multipaned windows sported yellow bric-a-brac trim and the roof of the porch shaded the yard like the brim of a floppy straw hat.

Jenna turned into the brick driveway and parked

the car. A petite figure in a polka-dot housedress launched out of a wicker chair on the porch and clattered down the steps to meet her.

"Mrs. Bunker?"

"It's Gabby to my friends, dear." Nutmeg brown eyes sparkled up at her beneath a cap of snow-white hair as high as the meringue on Kate's lemon custard pie. "Wes said I would like you. And you're right on time. Punctuality is so important, don't you agree?"

Gabby didn't wait for an answer as she marched Jenna up the narrow sidewalk. "Where are those delightful children Wes told me about?"

"They're with Kate this morning," Jenna said. "There's a special activity day for the children at church."

"Kate is a wonder. A *wonder.* I don't know what this town would do without her." Gabby nudged Jenna toward one of the wicker chairs. "And I don't know what I'd do without you."

"Without me?"

"I was so worried about my column. God and I had a talk about it last week and he said, Gabby my dear girl, you know you can trust me. If I can calm a storm, I can find a replacement for you." Gabby leaned forward. "And here you are!"

Yes, here I am, Jenna thought. With the speech she'd rehearsed on the drive over dissolving like the sugar cubes that Gabby was dropping into a glass of iced tea.

She cleared her throat. "I told Mr. Collins that I wasn't sure how long I would be in Mirror Lake. It might be better if you found someone more reliable to step in while you're gone."

Gabby slipped on the pair of rhinestone-studded spectacles dangling from a gold chain around her neck. Stared straight into Jenna's eyes. "Aren't you reliable?"

"Of course I am. But what if I have to leave?"

"We'll take it one day at a time. That's all any of us can do, isn't it? I've been writing my column since I retired from teaching. Everyone told me it was time to rest, but God had other plans. I decided I wasn't going to waste the time he gives me. People said I was off my rocker and there it was. The answer to my prayer. Not only did God give me a new purpose, he named it."

Jenna's confusion must have shown because Gabby laughed.

"Off my rocker. That's the name of my column, didn't Wes tell you?"

"He left that part out."

"I came up with the idea because everyone thinks that when a body retires, all that's left is the rocker on the front porch. I don't intend to be one of them."

From what Jenna could see, Gabby didn't need

to worry about that. The tiny frame packed more energy than a stick of dynamite. She reminded Jenna of Miss Franklin, her freshman English teacher. Miss Franklin had been the first one to notice that she had a natural gift for creative writing. The first one to encourage Jenna to enter the contest that had opened the door to a college scholarship…and encouraged her dream of becoming a writer.

"The stories I write don't come to me, I go to the stories. Interview interesting people in the area. Last week it was Emma Sutton. Sweet young woman. She wants to open a gallery for local artists."

Jenna had seen some of Emma's mosaics in Abby's garden at the bed-and-breakfast and the woman definitely had a gift.

"Someone has to convince our young people they don't have to leave the minute the ink dries on their high school diploma," Gabby snapped a linen cloth off the table with the flare of a magician and unveiled a plate of fist-sized homemade cookies. The aroma of warm chocolate and vanilla scented the air.

Jenna suddenly got the feeling that she was being bribed.

"So, what do you say?"

Cookie notwithstanding, there was only one thing that Jenna *could* say if she wanted Marlene, her boss, to let her stay in Mirror Lake a few more days.

"All right. One column at a time," Jenna agreed.

"Good, good. I'll tell Wes you'll have it on his desk by next Tuesday. I'll rest a lot easier knowing that's taken care of. Don't want to disappoint my readers."

Neither did Jenna.

"I'll interview the next person on your list."

"Wonderful." Gabby clapped her hands together and then slid the plate of cookies toward her. "Help yourself. I made these this morning."

"Do you have someone in mind for next week's edition?"

"As a matter of fact." A smile bowed Gabby's lips. "A local wildlife photographer. Stubborn fellow. Up until now, he hasn't agreed to an interview."

A prickle of suspicion ticked the back of Jenna's neck. "How many times have you asked him?"

"Only once or twice…a month. But I have a feeling he won't say no this time. Especially if you wear a pretty dress."

"Gabby!"

"It's true."

Jenna wasn't so sure. Gabby lived in Mirror Lake. If the man had turned her down why would he suddenly change his mind and allow Jenna to interview him?

"Why doesn't he want to be interviewed?"

"Well, he doesn't come to town very often. Lives in a cabin all by himself. Very mysterious. Has a reputation as being a bit of a recluse."

Which kind? Jenna wanted to ask. The harmless recluse who talked to the flora and fauna or the one that greeted visitors with a shotgun resting across his arm?

"Maybe I should start with someone else. I mean, if he doesn't want to be bothered…"

"Oh, he's just a little shy." Gabby brushed aside the suggestion. "And if you can convince him to agree to an interview it will be quite the feather in your cap. Wes might consider offering you a permanent position with the *Register.*"

Jenna choked back a laugh. She didn't *need* a feather in her cap. And she didn't need a job with the *Register,* either. She did, however, want to keep the one she had now.

"Is there something special about him?"

"I don't know about that, but there's certainly something special about his photographs. He manages to be in the right place at the right time and takes these impossible shots."

The right place at the right time.

Jenna had heard those words before.

I guess that sometimes a person is in the right place at the right time.

No, it couldn't be.

"Does he sell his photographs locally? *If—*" Jenna pressed down lightly on the word "*—he* agrees to an interview, I'd like to know something about his work before I meet him."

"You wouldn't recognize it even if he did. I've been told that he signs each one with a scripture reference instead of his name. Likes to keep a low profile. Humble. Gotta admire a man like that."

Jenna swallowed hard. It couldn't be a coincidence.

The photograph of the eagle in Dev's cabin had had a scripture verse in the corner. He'd quoted it to her. And the raw beauty of the scene had remained stuck in Jenna's mind for days.

What were the chances the photographer actually lived in the area?

Anticipation shimmied up Jenna's spine.

Maybe the guy would let her tag along the next time he went on a shoot. She could kill two birds with one stone. Step in for Gabby at the *Register* and write about her experience with a reclusive wildlife photographer for *Twin City Trends*. Marlene would love it and hopefully, so would her readers.

"I'll give him a call."

"That's the ticket." Gabby slapped her knee. "I knew we'd make a good team. You and I are both officially 'Off Our Rocker.'"

Unfortunately that was probably true, Jenna

thought, whipping out the notebook and pen she kept in her purse.

"So, what is this reclusive wildlife photographer's name?"

Gabby fed a piece of her cookie to the sleek Siamese cat that brushed against her ankles.

"It's McGuire. Devlin McGuire."

Chapter Fifteen

"What's the matter with you today?"

Dev glanced down at Violet. Ordinarily, the moment he pulled out his duffle bag, the dog planted herself in the passenger side of the vehicle, ready to embark on their next adventure. This morning she'd been constantly underfoot, tracking his every movement.

"Where's your ball?" Dev planned to throw it as far into the woods as he could, just to escape her mournful expression.

Violet flopped down at his feet with a sigh. And then proceeded to gnaw on the edge of the braided rug.

"It's only for a few days," Dev said, wondering just who he was trying to reassure.

He wasn't anticipating this trip as he had others in the past, either, which only proved how necessary it was. The conversation he'd had with Jenna continued to linger in his thoughts. So had the way she'd felt in his arms.

Dev hadn't meant to reach out to her in that way. But it had felt…right. And for a moment, Jenna had accepted his embrace. Leaned into it.

The emotions she stirred inside of him were confusing. In fact, when Dev looked at her, he was no longer reminded of Elaina. He saw…Jenna. Beautiful. Independent. Vulnerable.

Dangerous.

"Another reason to take off for a few days," he muttered.

Violet whined.

Dev tossed a pair of jeans into his duffle bag. "Don't argue with me—"

She ignored him instead. Rolled to her feet and padded out of the bedroom, plumed tail swinging. A few seconds later, Dev heard a rap on the sliding glass door.

Jenna and the children stood on the deck. Violet's nose was pressed against the glass, a tennis ball clamped between her teeth, her mood radically improved.

So had Dev's. No doubt about it. He was in trouble. Big trouble.

He slid open the door. "Good morning."

"I'm sorry to disturb you." Jenna seemed strangely ill at ease. Obviously this wasn't a social call.

Something twisted in Dev's gut. Had she decided to leave Mirror Lake before her sister returned? Because of his knuckle-headed move?

"You're not disturbing me." Disrupting his sleep, yes. Distracting him from his work, no doubt about it.

"Can we play with Violet?" Logan asked with a pleading look at his aunt.

"It's up to Dev."

"Please. She's been driving me crazy all morning."

Logan grinned down at the dog. "Where's your ball? Where is it?"

The dog, who'd been close to catatonic the past hour, practically performed a triple axel and soared off the end of the deck. Logan and Tori scrambled to catch up to her.

"Are you sure we're not interrupting anything?"

Dev pictured the half-packed duffle bag on the end of the bed. Silently tallied the number of hours of natural light left in the part of the national forest he planned to explore that afternoon.

"Nothing important. Would you like a cup of coffee?"

Jenna nodded.

Okay, now Dev knew something was wrong. Last night, she couldn't get away from him fast enough.

"Go ahead and grab a chair on the deck. I'll bring it out."

By the time he returned, Jenna had settled into one of the Adirondack chairs on the deck and was watching Logan and Tori take turns throwing the ball for Violet.

"Thank you," Jenna murmured when Dev set a steaming mug in front of her.

Dev dropped into the chair opposite her. "What's wrong?" he asked bluntly, unable to sit through anymore small talk.

"Wes Collins asked if I would be willing to take over Gabby Bunker's column while she has surgery."

"And you said yes?" The words were out before Dev could stop them.

"As a matter of fact, I didn't. I told Wes that I wasn't going to be in Mirror Lake very long, but I don't think he heard me." Jenna sighed. "And when I talked to Gabby, she didn't seem to hear me, either."

Dev grinned. "Maybe that's why the *Register* hasn't closed its doors like a lot of the other weekly newspapers."

"You read Gabby's column?"

"Not really."

The irrepressible reporter had been after him for the last five years to agree to an interview. And Dev had turned her down every time. Dev wasn't proud of the man he'd been. The only thing people knew about him was that he was a photographer.

Dev didn't want anyone poking into his past, asking questions he didn't want to answer.

"She likes to interview people who have a special talent of some kind."

Dev settled back in the chair. "So, who's your first victim?"

Jenna looked him straight in the eye.

"You are."

"No."

Jenna wished that Dev had looked stunned. Bewildered would have been acceptable, too. Because the stubborn set of his jaw only confirmed Gabby's claim.

Dev McGuire *was* the reclusive wildlife photographer who'd taken the photograph Jenna had seen in his living room the day he'd invited them over for supper.

That's why he'd been able to quote the verse from Psalms. He'd *chosen* it.

He could have answered all her questions about the photograph if he'd simply told her that he'd been the one who captured the shot.

So why hadn't he? He'd noticed how impressed she was. Why not take advantage of it and brag a little?

He'd let her think that he was unemployed.

No, she'd *assumed.* Jenna hadn't come right out and asked Dev what he did for a living because she hadn't wanted to put him on the spot.

Or had it been easier to believe that he was like her father? A drifter. A man who came and went on a whim.

As she'd driven to Church of Pines to pick up Tori and Logan, Jenna had sifted through their previous conversations. That's when she remembered the day Logan had caught Fred—the fish responsible for the chaos in her professional life.

She'd instructed a professional photographer—a very *successful* photographer if what Gabby had said was correct—on the finer points of taking a photograph.

Jenna was surprised Dev hadn't burst out laughing. But no, he'd stood patiently during her tutorial.

Now she had to get him to agree to the interview. Remember that she was a professional.

And forget what it had felt like to be in his arms.

Jenna hoped Dev would think her cheeks were turning pink from the sun.

"I know Gabby has asked you before—"

"At least once a month for the last five years," Dev interrupted. "She also tried to bribe me with chocolate chip cookies." His eyes rolled toward the sky. "I can't imagine who would fall for that."

Jenna didn't blink. "Neither can I."

"I'm not granting an interview."

"She asked me to call you before I call Hank the chainsaw artist."

Dev didn't look flattered. "I can't."

Jenna frowned at his choice of words. "Why not?"

"I could ask you the same thing."

"Well, you have a career that people find interesting—" He snorted. "And you brought this on yourself, you know," Jenna added irritably.

"What?"

"You've lived here for years and no one knows anything about you. You're mysterious. People *love* mysterious. You're the handsome recluse—" Jenna inwardly slapped herself. She hadn't really said the word *handsome*. Had she?

His lips twitched. *"Recluse?"*

"That's what Gabby called you." Jenna didn't think the label fit. A true recluse would have resented their arrival. Wouldn't have befriended Logan and intervened on his behalf about the canoe trip.

"It makes people curious about you. They start to speculate about the reason you moved to Mirror Lake. Why you don't sell your work in local galleries. Why you don't attend community functions."

"This is *why* I don't attend community functions. I don't want people like Gabby Bunker digging around…" Dev's jaw locked, severing the rest of the sentence.

"Unless you have some deep dark secret, I don't see the problem."

A shadow passed through Dev's eyes, causing Jenna to pause.

Did he have some deep, dark secret?

"I don't understand why you agreed to fill in for Gabby. I didn't think you planned to be in Mirror Lake for more than a week."

Dev had neatly turned the tables on her.

She couldn't admit that she was getting pressure from her own editor.

"I caved when Gabby brought out the chocolate chip cookies, okay?"

A smile curved Dev's lips. Jenna pressed her advantage.

"It's a human interest piece," she said. "And like it or not, you are an interesting human."

"I'll do an interview on two conditions," he finally said.

The sudden glint in those amber eyes set off an internal alarm system. "What conditions?"

"Number one, I come up with the list of questions, not you."

"That's not the way it's done."

"It's the way *this* is done." Dev had the audacity to smile.

"Fine." Jenna bit down on the word. "Number two?"

"You give Logan permission to go on the canoe trip."

It was the last thing Jenna expected him to say.

And it immediately brought up a memory that she had been trying so hard to suppress. Dev gently drawing her into his arms, murmuring words of encouragement in her ear, lending her his strength.

"I'll...think about it."

"And I'll think about the interview."

How had she gotten herself into this situation? Because of her inability to disappoint a persistent senior citizen and a weakness for chocolate chip cookies.

And, if she were completely honest with herself, a crazy, inexplicable desire to get to know a mysterious recluse better!

"All right," Jenna said slowly. "But I have a condition, too."

"You can't put a condition on my condition."

The lift of her chin said she could. "The canoe trip is for guys, so someone—a *guy* someone—will have to go with him. Kate mentioned that Alex is going back to Chicago to meet with his attorney about the sale of his hotels so I don't think he'll be available that day. You'll have to go with him."

"Me?"

"It was your idea."

"Fine." He borrowed Jenna's favorite word.

"Really?" The surprise on her face told Dev he'd given in too easily.

And maybe he had.

First he'd agreed to be interviewed for a news-paper article—no, he'd agreed to let *Jenna* inter-view him for a newspaper article—and now he'd offered to take Logan on a daylong canoe trip.

"I can go on the canoe trip?" Feet thudded against the deck, startling both him and Jenna. "With Dev?"

Dev hadn't realized Logan was within earshot when he'd made the offer to accompany him.

"Do you still want to go?" Dev hedged.

"I can't wait to tell Cody and Jeremy!"

Well, that answered his question.

"I wanna go, too." Tori sat down on Jenna's lap and snuggled against her.

Dev watched Jenna wrap her arms around her niece and brush a wayward strand of hair off Tori's face. How could she think she wasn't good for these kids? Jenna might not have seen them for seven years but it was obvious she loved them.

"This canoe trip is just for boys," Jenna said.

"That's not fair!"

"Sometimes we girls plan things that don't in-clude the boys."

Tori tipped her head. "Like a special tea party?"

"That certainly qualifies."

"Can we invite Kate? And Abby? And Lady and Mulligan?"

Jenna looked a little dazed at the speed in which

her idea was growing. "I suppose so…but probably not Lady and Mulligan."

"But Violet will need a friend to play with." Tori reached out and patted the dog's massive head. "She can't go in the canoe with Dev and Logan. She won't fit."

Jenna looked at Dev, who locked down a laugh. "That's true."

"So she has to stay with us."

Dev hadn't thought about Violet. And judging from the panicked look Jenna tossed in his direction, neither had she.

"I'm sure Violet would much rather attend the tea party." Dev tried to keep a straight face.

"Or you could get a bigger canoe," Jenna suggested sweetly.

Violet rested her chin on Jenna's knee and whined. To Dev's amazement, she patted the dog's head.

"All right, all right." She laughed. "You're invited to the tea party—but you can't sit at the table."

Dev stared at Jenna, captivated by the music of her laughter. And the subtle changes he saw.

For a moment, their eyes met and Dev's heart shifted into second gear.

"I suppose that going along on a photo shoot is out of the question?"

Dev didn't hesitate. "Yes."

"Does it have something to do with the mystery surrounding the reclusive Dev McGuire?"

Dev smiled.

"I ask the questions, remember?"

Chapter Sixteen

"Devlin actually agreed to the interview?" Gabby shouted the words, causing Jenna to wince and move the cell phone a little further from her ear.

"Yes, he did." Jenna couldn't believe it, either.

The elderly reporter chuckled. "I had a feeling he wouldn't be able to turn you down."

Jenna wasn't going to touch that one. And she wasn't going to mention Dev's conditions, either. Logan had been ecstatic that he could go on the canoe trip, but Jenna had sensed Dev's reluctance.

Why didn't he want to be interviewed?

She stepped over the frontier town and walked to the window. Tori had set up a tea party under the oak in the front yard while Logan patrolled the perimeter, looking for animal tracks.

"We'll be setting up a time to meet within the next few days." Jenna's stomach dipped at the thought of seeing Dev again. "I'll give you a copy to proof before I turn it in."

"That's very sweet of you, but we both know it isn't necessary," Gabby said gently. "I skimmed through a few issues of *Twin City Trends*. God has given you a special gift, my dear."

"Thank you." Jenna had won several awards but for some reason, none of them had meant more to her than this woman's praise.

"I have a doctor's appointment in a few minutes so I better scoot. I'm glad you called and told me the news. It made my day."

"Do you need anything else, Gabby?" Jenna hesitated. "I mean, do you have someone to drive you home from the hospital after your surgery?"

"Oh my goodness, you don't need to worry about that." Gabby chuckled. "I'm going to have meals brought right to my front door for the next two weeks and help with my housework and cutting the grass."

"Your family takes good care of you."

"I don't have any family left. It's my other family that's chipping in to help."

"Your other family?"

"The family of God." Gabby sounded surprised that Jenna didn't know what she was talking about. "We're supposed to look out for one another. Bear one another's burdens, you know."

No, Jenna didn't know. But she'd experienced

it when Kate and her friends had shown up and helped transformed the dreary cabin into a home.

Apparently Gabby believed it, too. And so did Dev.

You don't have to do this alone, you know.

"But I wouldn't be against a visitor or two while I'm recuperating," Gabby was saying. "I can't wait to hear how the interview goes."

"You're incorrigible, Gabby."

"Why thank you, dear."

Jenna laughed and hung up the phone. Before she had a chance to put it down on the table, it rang again.

"Did you change your mind about proofing the article already?" she teased.

Silence stretched on the other end of the line.

"Jenna?"

Jenna collapsed into the closest chair before her knees gave out. "Shelly?"

A shaky laugh followed. "Yeah, it's me. The counselor said you called."

Three times, Jenna was tempted to say. "I wanted to find out how you're doing."

"Okay, I guess." Shelly sounded distracted. "The first few days were the worst. And they won't let me smoke."

"That's probably a good thing." Jenna's gaze drifted to the colorful rug on the floor that Abby had put down to cover the burn.

"I guess." There was an edge in Shelly's voice that hadn't been there before. "Where are you? In Minneapolis?"

The question confused Jenna. "No, I'm in Mirror Lake. With Tori and Logan."

"I suppose you found that little bed-and-breakfast up the road? It's probably more your style."

Jenna let the comment slide. "We're staying at the cabin. Tori and Logan are more comfortable here."

Shelly snorted. "Not exactly the Ritz, is it?"

Jenna's gaze settled on the rug that Abby had given her. The cotton candy-pink afghan that the Knit Our Hearts Together ministry had given to Tori.

"It's got potential." She repeated Abby's words. "How are the kids doing?"

"Would you like to talk to them?" Jenna offered. "They're playing outside but I can call them in. I'm sure they'd love to hear your voice."

"No, don't bother them. I can call back another time."

Outside, a peal of childish laughter pierced the air. Logan was giving one of Tori's stuffed animals a piggyback ride around the yard.

You're missing this, Shelly, she thought. *And they're missing you.*

An awkward silence swelled between them. They should have so many things to catch up on.

So much to say. It had been easier to talk to the cashier at the grocery store than have a conversation with her own sister.

"How long do you think you'll be at New Day?"

"The counselor recommended I stay another week or two."

Jenna drew in a breath. Released it. "Shelly, I'd like you to think about coming back to Minneapolis. All three of you. There's a great school about a block from where I live and—"

"Didn't we already have this conversation?" Shelly interrupted. "Like, seven years ago?"

"Yes, we did." *And if you'd listened to me, maybe your life would have been different.* "I've been worried about you."

"Look, I'm glad you came to save the day," Shelly said with a weary sigh. "And I'm sorry for what happened. I know I messed up big time. Tell Logan and Tori that I promise things will be different when I get home."

I promise.

Jenna closed her eyes. Didn't Shelly realize she was parroting their mother's favorite phrase. And nothing had ever changed. They'd still moved from town to town, driven by Nola's restlessness and discontent. It was as if their mother had always been searching for some elusive treasure just beyond her reach.

"I'm glad you're getting help," Jenna said softly. "Logan and Tori need you."

"Everyone needs something." Shelly's voice carried a disturbing undercurrent of bitterness. "Sometimes it gets to be too much, you know?"

"Shelly—"

"Listen, my time is up, and I have to make another call."

Jenna didn't have time to protest. To ask the questions that had continued to mount since she'd arrived in Mirror Lake. What had happened with Vance? What were Shelly's plans for the future? For Tori and Logan?

Jenna hung up the phone and felt a tear slide down her cheeks. She'd dreamed of this moment for years. Reconnecting with the only remaining member of her family, the sister she'd once been so close to.

But the conversation was a harsh reminder that she didn't know Shelly at all. It was almost worse than seven years of silence.

The cabin's walls suddenly felt as if they were closing in on her.

Jenna slipped outside. The scent of rain weighted the air and gray clouds inched toward the sun, threatening to snuff out the sunny afternoon. Except that Shelly's call had already accomplished that.

"Want some tea, Aunt Jenna?" Tori held up her toy teapot.

Jenna sat down beside her and accepted a plastic cup stuffed with blades of grass. "It smells wonderful."

Tori smiled. "It's got two sugar cubes in it. See?"

Jenna saw two acorns rolling around the bottom of the cup. "Just the way I like it."

"I made something for you. You can wear it when we have our special tea next Saturday." Tori pulled a bracelet from the pocket of her shorts. Three strands of yarn—pink, of course—loosely braided together.

"It's beautiful." Jenna pulled Tori into her lap and tickled her sides. "And. So. Are. You."

Tori giggled. "Put it on!"

"You're going to have to help me. Can you tie a bow?"

"Uh-huh. Logan taught me how. He's a good brother."

"Yes, he is." Jenna felt a tightening in her chest as she held out her wrist so Tori could tie the ends together. She regretted letting Shelly end the conversation without talking to her about the children. Her sister had always been a "live for the moment" type of girl, while Jenna preferred to plan for the future.

How could she get Shelly to realize that her behavior wasn't only affecting herself, it was affecting Tori and Logan, too?

Logan dashed up to her. "Can we go for a walk, Aunt Jenna?"

Jenna figured it was an excuse to play with Violet, but she didn't want to interrupt Dev twice in one day. Or give him an opportunity to change his mind about the interview.

"How about a short one? I think it's going to rain."

They helped Tori pick up her toys and stash them on the porch. Jenna kept a wary eye on the tufts of dark clouds that drifted past, carried by the breeze that skipped over the lake.

Logan stopped several times to show her things that he'd discovered on one of his expeditions. A snail attached to a lily pad. A cocoon knit to the wooden post of the dock. A scattering of footprints in the soft ground near the edge of the woods, evidence that the doe and her twins had visited during the night.

One name kept popping up as Logan led Jenna and Tori on his treasure hunt.

Dev.

He'd been the one to point out those little things the night he'd taken them on that impromptu field trip. Jenna had assumed Dev's attention to detail had been honed by living in the woods, never dreaming it was because he was a professional photographer.

A. Professional. Photographer.

Jenna closed her eyes.

It explained so many things. Why he traveled so much. Why he was so comfortable in the outdoors.

But it didn't explain why an entire town had branded him a recluse. Jenna had been more concerned with sticking to boundaries than Dev had.

"Look, Aunt Jenna!" Logan rushed up to her, hands cupped, water draining from between his fingers. "I found it in the water."

She drew back. "Is it alive?"

"Uh-huh." Logan's eyes were shining. "It's a crayfish. A big one."

Of course it was. Jenna was beginning to think that God had supersized every creature around here.

"They're easy to catch. Do you want to try?"

Jenna hadn't realized they'd wandered so far down the shoreline. In fact, they were closer to Dev's cabin than they were to their own.

Lightning flickered in the underbelly of a dark cloud rolling toward the lake.

"I think it's time to head back."

Thunder rumbled in the distance and Tori clapped her hands over her ears. "I don't like storms."

"Come on." Jenna made a decision. She took the children by the hand and they sprinted for the deck where she and Dev had had coffee that morning.

There were no signs of life. No lights in the windows. No Violet barking out a greeting.

"It doesn't look like anyone's home."

Logan peered through the sliding glass doors. "Dev probably left already."

Jenna brushed a raindrop off her cheek and looked at her nephew. "Left?"

"Uh-huh. He has to take some pictures but he'll be back in a few days."

The numbness spreading through Jenna's limbs wasn't caused by the cold rain pelting her skin. It was disappointment. She'd been hoping Dev would be home. Wanted to tell him that Shelly had called.

Jenna had been so afraid that Logan would come to depend on Dev that she hadn't considered the possibility that she would, too.

"You might have to move. Mirror Lake is now officially on the map."

"I have no idea what you mean, Talia, but talk fast." Dev propped the phone against his ear as he set another tent stake in place while keeping a wary eye on the clouds boiling in the sky above him. "I'm about to get caught in a downpour and I can't believe there's cell phone reception here."

"You always say that."

"This time it's true." He'd just hiked ten miles into the heart of the national forest.

"Your little town is featured on a website this week. A friend of mine told me about it."

"How did that happen?"

"It's in *Twin City Trends*. A pretty cute article about a fish named Fred. There's a picture, too. I'll read the headline. 'City Girl Goes Country.' Jenna Gardner wrote it."

Dev rocked back on his heels, the approaching storm momentarily overshadowed by a sudden turbulence inside of him.

"Jenna Gardner?"

"Have you met her?" Talia asked.

He must have been silent too long.

"Yes." Met her. Laughed with her. Held her in his arms. "She's only in town for another week or so."

"Does she know who you are?" Talia demanded.

"She knows I'm a photographer." *Thank you, Gabby Bunker.*

"Are you sure?" Talia was no longer teasing. "How can she work for *Trends* and not know who you are?"

"I'm not Brad Pitt, Talia. What I am—" Dev grabbed another stake. "—is old news."

"I'm not so sure about that. If I were you, I'd steer clear of her."

"I think it might be a little late for that." Dev winced as a raindrop splashed against his hand.

"Why?"

"I already agreed to an interview."

Dev heard a crash. "What was that?"

"You owe me…new coffee mug…bought it…
London. What do you mean…agreed…inter-
view?"

Dev was only picking up every second or third
word. They were either losing the connection or
Talia had started to hyperventilate.

"All Jenna knows is that I live in a cabin and
take photographs of fuzzy little creatures." Dev
ignored the snort of disbelief following the ab-
breviated description of his chosen career. "She's
writing the article for the local newspaper."

"Until she decides to research her latest sub-
ject. You value your privacy and someone like
Jenna Gardner would love to have her byline on
the 'where is Dev McGuire now' story. Do you
want someone like her to dig up the past?"

"I don't have anything to hide."

Except maybe one thing.

He'd fallen for the girl next door.

Chapter Seventeen

"So this is where you've been hiding."

"Caitlin!" Jenna yanked open the door. "What are you doing here?"

Caitlin Walsh grinned. "My hubby has a book signing in Chicago this weekend, so the kids and I are heading up to Cooper's Landing to spend the weekend with their grandpa. Mirror Lake is only a few miles out of the way, so here we are."

"I'm glad you stopped by." Jenna felt tears poke the backs of her eyes. She hadn't realized how nice it would be to see a familiar face. Jenna had met the image consultant while working together on the magazine's annual makeover issue and she'd been drawn to the young woman's drive and commitment.

Over the past year, what had started as a professional relationship had gradually turned into a friendship. The first real one that Jenna had ever had. Although Caitlin was a busy wife and mother, they still found time to meet for lunch once a week.

"Someone had to check up on you." Caitlin flipped a swatch of dark hair over her shoulder. "I didn't trust Dawn to give me reliable updates."

Dawn. Jenna didn't want to be reminded how her coworker had tried to sabotage her column.

Caitlin's indigo eyes widened when she looked over Jenna's shoulder. "I passed an adorable bed-and-breakfast a few miles back and you're staying here?"

"Logan and Tori have been shuffled around a lot over the past few weeks. I thought it might be better if they stayed in familiar surroundings while we got to know each other better."

"You've got a pretty view of the lake." Caitlin smiled. "All these trees remind me of Cooper's Landing."

"How long can you stay?" Jenna asked.

"If Josh and Brady find out the fish are biting, we might be here all weekend!"

Jenna had met the twins when Caitlin stopped by her office one day. The boys and their sister were from Caitlin's husband's first marriage to model Ashleigh Heath, who had died in a plane crash. He'd been raising the children on his own when he'd met Caitlin through, of all things, *Twin City Trends* annual makeover contest. Caitlin's new daughter, who'd been twelve at the time, had submitted an application without her father knowing about it and brought Caitlin, the image consultant who judged the contest, to their front door.

Jenna followed her friend outside. All the children had gathered at the edge of the water to admire Logan's crayfish—Tori had named him Eddie—which had been transported to a comfortable new home in an old minnow trap.

In the few minutes since their arrival, the children had already gotten acquainted. Josh and Brady had already kicked off their Nikes and were wading in the shallow water, helping Logan find a friend for Eddie.

"You have a great family," Jenna murmured as they made their way back to the cabin.

"So do you."

They might be Jenna's family…but they were Shelly's children. In the end, Jenna knew that her sister would have the final say when it came to Tori and Logan's future. Their last conversation had left Jenna feeling unsettled as to whether she would make the right one.

"Shelly will be home soon."

Caitlin gave her a thoughtful look. "So what happens after that? You go back to the city? Back to life as you once knew it?"

"I don't think going back is ever an option," Jenna said slowly. "I think I'll be trying to figure out a way to move forward again." Without Logan and Tori.

Without Dev.

"The kids seem pretty happy here," Caitlin observed as she settled into a chair on the porch. "And so does their aunt."

"I'm happy in the city. I've got a nice apartment. A career that I love." Jenna had worked hard for all those things. She loved being independent. Respected. Every week, she gave other young women advice about how to make their mark in the world. How to get noticed.

"Hey! Earth to Jenna!" Caitlin teased. "Where did you go?"

"Sorry. What did you say?"

"I read your blog."

Jenna shook her head. "Dawn posted that without my knowledge."

"I thought so. But it was really funny. Different from the way you usually write."

"Marlene thought so, too. She wants me to write another one." Jenna told Caitlin about Wes Collins and filling in for Gabby Bunker.

"Off My Rocker?" Caitlin sputtered. "Are you kidding me?"

"It fits, doesn't it?" Jenna laughed. "But Gabby's an amazing woman. I hope I have that much pep when I'm eighty years old."

"So, who does she want you to interview?"

"Believe it or not, my next-door neighbor."

"Are you—" Caitlin leaned forward in the chair "—blushing?"

"No." Was she?

"Is this a male neighbor or a female neighbor?" Caitlin demanded.

"Male."

"You *are* blushing!"

"It's eighty degrees," Jenna pointed out. "And I didn't set up the interview, Gabby did. She's been pestering him for years to agree to an interview. He's a wildlife photographer."

"And he's your neighbor. Have you been spending a lot of time together?"

"He invited us over for supper one evening. And he took us on a hike." And listened to her pour out her heart.

"I'm pretty sure that qualifies as spending time together."

"The kids kind of brought us together," Jenna explained before Caitlin got any crazy ideas. "He's great with them, especially Logan."

"Mmm."

"Don't get any ideas. Dev McGuire is happy in his little cabin on the lake—"

"Dev McGuire?" Caitlin interrupted.

"That's right." Jenna saw a change in her friend's expression. "Is something wrong?"

"I'm sorry, it's just that I knew a Dev McGuire, but it can't possibly be the same person."

"Why not?"

"Because I'm pretty sure this one wouldn't be living in a cabin in northern Wisconsin. I volunteered at a charity bachelor auction before you worked at *Trends,* and Dev McGuire was the hot ticket of the evening. He was also the most arrogant man I've had the displeasure of working with." Caitlin shook her head. "He's the kind of guy who needed to buy two plane tickets when he went on a trip. One for him and one for his ego."

"Caitlin!"

"It's true." Her friend flashed a grin. "The McGuire family still owns the largest construction and design firm in the Twin Cities. The family was country club royalty, and Dev was being groomed to take over the kingdom when his father retired. He would have done a good job. Dev was brilliant and handsome and ambitious."

"If you like that kind of guy," Jenna teased.

"Everyone seemed to," Caitlin said drily. "From what I witnessed, he welcomed the attention. Dev had a reputation as a self-centered player. Pia Thornton, the woman who won the date with him called the auction committee a few weeks later and complained that he'd stood her up."

"Ouch."

"He was engaged to a client of mine, Elaina

Hammond, but she ended up canceling the wedding about a month before they exchanged vows."

"What happened?"

"Elaina complained that Dev had changed. At the time I remember wondering why she considered that a bad thing!"

"You're right. It can't be the same man," Jenna said, unable to hide her relief. "My Dev McGuire cares more about who a person is than what they do."

"*Your* Dev McGuire?"

"I didn't say that."

"Oh, yes. You did." Caitlin's eyes sparkled. "Here I am, trying to set you up with eligible bachelors all over the Twin Cities and you go and fall for the guy next door."

"That's ridiculous, Caitlin, I haven't fallen for anyone! I hardly know him."

"It sounds to me like you know the important things," Caitlin said, way too cheerfully for Jenna's peace of mind. "From the way you described him, the guy is a real sweetheart. Good with kids. Likes animals. Tall, dark and a little mysterious."

Jenna felt a trickle of unease coast down her spine.

"What happened to Dev McGuire?" she asked slowly. "Does he still live in Minneapolis?"

"I don't know where he's living now." Caitlin toyed with the metal bracelets circling her wrist, a birthday gift from her sister, Meghan. "He dropped off the grid about five years ago."

Five years. It had to be another coincidence.

"Why?" Ordinarily, Jenna wouldn't have pushed. Having been the brunt of gossip while growing up, she tended to avoid it. But the troubled expression on Caitlin's face caused a prickle of alarm to slide down Jenna's spine.

"You know how people talk." Her friend shrugged. "It was a rumor, that's all."

Jenna leaned forward. "What kind of rumor?"

"That Dev McGuire was responsible for his brother's death."

Jenna's pulse spiked—until she remembered that they weren't talking about the same man.

"That's terrible. How—"

"Mom!" Brady clattered onto the porch. "I saw a wolf! It's *huge*. Gray-and-brown—"

"With a pink collar," Jenna finished. "Her name is Violet."

And the dog's presence could only mean one thing. Dev had returned.

"Cool! I'm going to tell Josh." Brady took off to find his twin brother.

"Don't worry." Jenna saw Caitlin frown. "Violet might be the size of a Volkswagen Bug, but she doesn't bite."

"It's not them I'm worried about." Caitlin brushed aside her concern with a sweep of her manicured hand. "The boys can be a little over-whelming. They treat every dog they meet as a potential wrestling partner."

The sharp whistle that pierced the air and fused Jenna to the chair had the opposite effect on Caitlin.

"I guess this means I'm going to meet the guy next door," she teased, pushing to her feet to get a better look.

Dev had stopped to talk to Logan near the dock. He must have just returned from his trip because he wore the same camouflage fatigues he'd had on the day they'd met. The breeze ruffled his dark hair. He looked tan and fit and gorgeous and now Caitlin was looking at *her.*

"Wow." Caitlin blinked. "For a writer, you definitely need to work on your descriptions," she whispered to Jenna. "The guy is drop-dead gorgeous. And by the way, you're blushing again!"

Jenna wished she could deny it but she'd missed Dev the past few days. Worried about him when thunder had rumbled through the clouds and rain hammered the roof during the night.

"Violet's back!" Logan shouted, as if the two women standing on the porch had somehow missed a dog the size of a compact car.

Dev approached the cabin with his easy, loose-limbed stride. The warm smile he tossed in her direction melted all of Jenna's misgivings like cotton candy left out in the sun.

"Caitlin, this is my neighbor, Dev McGuire. Dev, my friend, Caitlin Walsh."

Jenna heard Caitlin draw in a quick breath at the same time she saw Dev's smile fade.

Judging from the expressions on their faces, the two had already met.

Dev didn't bother to extend his hand.

The stunning, dark-haired woman standing next to Jenna looked familiar but Dev couldn't quite remember why.

"I'm sorry—" Dev wasn't sure for what at the moment, but the flash of dislike in the woman's deep blue eyes clued him into the fact they'd met in a former life. *His* former life.

"Caitlin. My maiden name was McBride."

Dev put the first and last name together and came up with the answer. He'd met the image consultant briefly when their paths had crossed during one of *Twin City Trends* charity bachelor auctions.

It shouldn't have surprised Dev that Caitlin McBride Walsh and Jenna moved in the same social circles. The foundation of the image consultant's business were women like his mother and Elaina. And Jenna.

"Of course." Dev nodded. "It's been a few years."

Caitlin looked surprised and Dev realized she'd

expected him to come down with a swift and convenient form of amnesia.

"I wasn't expecting to see you here," she said, her blue eyes as frosty as her tone.

That makes two of us, Dev thought.

Caitlin linked her arm through Jenna's and the protective gesture burned its way through Dev, searing his conscience. The woman obviously hadn't forgotten the way he'd treated Pia Thornton, the young socialite who had won a dinner date with him.

Yeah, you were a real prize back then.

He glanced at Jenna, who looked more than a little bewildered by the exchange. Dev had no doubt Caitlin would fill her in the moment he left. Which he probably shouldn't delay any longer.

"I'm sorry for intruding." Dev stepped back and grabbed hold of Violet's collar, anticipating that his dog would be less than thrilled to be separated from Logan only moments after they'd arrived. "I just wanted to stop by and set up a time for the interview."

And he'd missed Jenna.

"Do you have to go already?" Tori's wide blue eyes stared up at him beseechingly and to Dev's astonishment, she lifted her arms.

Without thinking, Dev scooped up the little girl. Her chubby arms looped around his neck. "We missed you, didn't we, Aunt Jenna?"

Jenna made a sound that could have been interpreted any number of different ways.

"Are you going to stay for supper, too?"

"No, I have some unpacking to do." Dev shifted Tori onto his hip and reached into his shirt pocket. "But I found something I thought you might like."

"For me? What is it?"

"It's a hawk feather. I found it in an abandoned nest."

"It's pretty." Tori brushed the tip against her cheek. "Did you bring somethin' for Logan, too?"

"Tori!" Logan scraped the ground with the toe of his shoe. "You aren't supposed to ask."

"Then how are you s'posed to *know?*"

Even Caitlin smiled at the five-year-old's logic.

"Of course I did." Dev fished around inside his pocket again.

"An arrowhead!" Logan's eyes got wide as he ran his thumb along the notches in the smooth stone. "I'm going to show Jeremy."

"It was thoughtful of you to bring them something," Jenna said stiffly.

"No problem." Dev had brought Jenna something, too, but there was no way he was going to give it to her with Caitlin Walsh looking on.

"Can I play with Violet later?" Logan wanted to know.

Dev felt as if there were a heavy weight on his

chest, pushing the air from his lungs. "That's up to your aunt."

But if Caitlin Walsh had anything to say about it, Jenna would probably never want to speak to him again.

Chapter Eighteen

Jenna collapsed into a chair on the porch and stared at the water with unseeing eyes.

She tried to reconcile the man she knew with the one that Caitlin had described. She couldn't. Something had changed him.

Before she'd left, Caitlin had asked if Jenna minded if she prayed with her. Jenna had blinked back tears while her friend thanked God for his many blessings. For the special people he brought into their lives. After the "amen," Caitlin had looked her right in the eye and told her that she thought Dev was one of them.

"The man I knew wouldn't have befriended a couple of neighbor kids and brought them a gift. And jeans and hiking boots?" Caitlin had pretended to shudder. *"He wouldn't have been caught dead in anything other than Armani."*

Caitlin's attempt at humor had drawn a faint

smile. But there was still one thing Jenna couldn't get past.

She'd asked Caitlin if she remembered Dev's brother's name.

It was Jason.

In her mind's eye, Jenna could see the expression on Dev's face when Logan had asked about the name etched on the telescope. Not guilt, but grief.

"Jenna?"

Jenna raised her head, wondering if she'd imagined Dev's voice. But there he was. Standing at the edge of the shadows.

She rose slowly to her feet.

"I'm here for my interview."

"Now?"

"I told you that I'd get back to you in a few days."

And he was a man who kept his promises.

"Dev." Jenna wasn't sure she was up to this. "You don't have to—"

"Yes, I do."

Jenna stared at her, trying to see the man that Caitlin had described. Self-centered. Arrogant. Ambitious.

She didn't know that person—but she knew this one.

"All right. We can sit on the porch. Logan and Tori are already asleep." Jenna wiped her damp palms down the front of her jeans. "Just give me a minute."

When Jenna returned, Dev was sitting on the swing, arms folded behind his head. How could he be so calm? Jenna's hands were trembling so hard she didn't trust them. She turned on a recording device and set it on the table between them.

"You first," Dev said.

"But…I thought you were going to come up with the questions."

"I changed my mind."

The man who'd done everything in his power to avoid the public eye was giving her control of the interview.

Why?

That was the first question Jenna wanted to ask. But she chose a standard one instead. A *safe* one.

"What made you choose a career as a wildlife photographer?"

"I didn't really choose it, it chose me." Dev shrugged. "A way to pass the time when I moved to Mirror Lake."

"And why did you move here?"

The porch swing creaked as Dev shifted. "I told you that my grandfather bought the cabin as an investment when I was about Logan's age. The original plan was to fix the place up and sell it— but then he surprised everyone and kept it. Every summer, my brother Jason and I would spend a

few weeks here, fishing and swimming and finding crawly things under the rocks."

Jenna thought of Logan.

"When I was in junior high, my dad decided
that my time would be better spent doing other
things, and I agreed with him. Jason kept coming
back, though. Nature fascinated him. He would
take our grandpa's old Polaroid and shoot up rolls
of film. I started to work on the ground floor of
the family business. Literally."

"McGuire Construction." Jenna had seen the
ads on television, the billboards, but if it hadn't
been for Caitlin, she'd have never connected Dev
to one of the most successful businesses in the
Twin Cities.

"Dad took it for granted that both of us would
eventually work for him, but he cut Jason some
slack because he was the youngest. He liked to
brag to his friends that it would take two of us to
replace him when he retired." Dev drove a hand
through his hair. "But Jason decided he wanted to
do something else with his life. Said that God had
another plan for him."

"Your dad didn't approve," Jenna guessed.

"Neither of us did. I gave him a hard time about
it. About everything. His decisions. His future. His
faith. I'm surprised Jason didn't stop talking to me."
A wry smile tipped the corner of Dev's lips. "There
were times I wish he *had*. His favorite topic was

his faith. Jason had always approached life from a different angle. Every day was an adventure."

"Like Logan," Jenna murmured. Now she understood why a man determined to keep himself apart from others had made room in his life for a lonely little boy.

"I thought Jason was crazy to give up everything but he would tell me that what he'd given up didn't compare to what he'd gained. We tend to avoid what we don't understand so I suppose it was inevitable that we drifted apart." Dev laughed, but there was no humor in it. "Jason went to work for a nonprofit ministry that built houses for underprivileged families while I turned neighborhoods into golf courses and condominiums.

"One day, out of the blue, he called and said he'd reserved a campsite in Michigan's Upper Peninsula. He reminded me that I'd promised to do the whole outdoor wilderness adventure thing with him some day and that if we didn't do it now, before—"

Dev paused and Jenna almost wished she hadn't known why. The interview was excavating enough painful memories.

She drew in a breath and released it.

"The wedding."

The quiet statement told Dev that Caitlin had provided the details about his life and then some.

Looking at Jenna now, Dev couldn't believe he'd actually compared her to Elaina when they first met. The two women were nothing alike.

Elaina wouldn't have been caught in the middle of a squirt gun fight or spent an afternoon combing the beach for crayfish. She and Jenna might have chosen the same designer for their wardrobe, but Elaina's beauty had been skin-deep. She'd lacked Jenna's warmth. Her sense of humor.

Although the thought had never crossed Dev's mind at the time, he'd often wondered if Elaina had loved the idea of being Mrs. Dev McGuire more than she'd loved *him*.

Jason had never come right out and said anything, but Dev sensed his brother didn't approve of Elaina. It had been another source of tension between them.

His parents, on the other hand, had welcomed Elaina with open arms. In fact, Dev suspected his mother had orchestrated their first meeting at a charity fundraiser. Naturally, they'd blamed him when Elaina broke their engagement.

"Did you know Elaina?"

"No, but Caitlin mentioned she was a former client."

Dev wasn't surprised but he didn't want to talk about Elaina anymore. "I agreed to go on the camping trip with Jason on one condition. That he wouldn't talk about God while we were there."

He could still picture Jason's wide grin.

Whatever you say, big brother, but he's right there with us, Dev. Whether I talk about him or not.

"On Saturday, Dad called and said that I needed to come back. Some software bigwig had flown in for the weekend and wanted our opinion on a new complex he was thinking about building in the area.

"Dad was a little upset that the guy insisted on talking to me instead of him." But Dev had been flattered. At the time, he remembered thinking that it could finally be the thing that tipped the balance of power in his favor. Prove beyond a doubt that Brent McGuire could hand the reins of the business over to his oldest son with no regrets.

"Jason and I argued. He tried to talk me into postponing the meeting for another day." Dev paused, unprepared for the grief that still had the power to strip the breath from his lungs.

"But you didn't," Jenna said softly.

"No." Only hundreds of times since, when Dev had tortured himself by reliving the moment he'd thrown his duffle bag in the trunk of the car and left his brother standing at the campsite alone. But not that day.

"While I was meeting with our potential

client, my brother hiked up the Porcupine Mountains by himself. I'm not sure why he didn't stay on the marked path—something must have caught his attention. But the ledge gave way and he...he fell." Dev hadn't been there, and yet he could see the ground crumble and break away. And Jason...

Jenna's slender fingers gripped his, giving Dev the strength to continue. "I'm so sorry," she whispered.

Dev stared down at the tape recorder between them, forced himself to tell her the rest of the story. "Two campers found Jason the next day and flagged down a warden. But it was too late."

"It wasn't your fault." Jenna's hand tightened. "You couldn't have known what would happen."

"But things would have been different if I'd been there."

"You can't be sure of that, either."

If only Jenna were right.

"Jason didn't die right away. He was injured and went into shock. It wasn't the fall that killed him—it was the fact that there was no one there when it happened. I wasn't there."

For the first time, Dev said the words out loud that had haunted him for the last five years.

Tears were streaming down Jenna's face. For a moment, they sat in complete silence, hands linked together.

"I thought Jason was wasting his time, building

houses for people who couldn't afford to pay for them. I was always looking for the next big deal. More toys. A flashier car. I didn't understand his faith, so I mocked it. I even teased him about his obsession with the outdoors. Jason loved being out in nature. He claimed God's handiwork was everywhere and it helped him get to know him better."

"Is that why you came to Mirror Lake after he died?"

"My parents thought I'd gone off the deep end. Elaina said if I walked away from the company, she would have to break our engagement. Said I didn't have anything to offer."

"She was wrong."

Jenna said the words so quietly that Dev thought he might have imagined them. "I wasn't planning to make it permanent. I just wanted to understand my brother…and to find God so I could yell at him. I think that secretly I was hoping a lightning bolt would strike me. I wanted God to punish me for not loving my brother more than I loved the idea of being president of McGuire Construction."

"I'm sure Jason knew that you loved him."

Dev wanted to believe Jenna was right. He'd clung to that thought more than once as the years slipped by. "When I got to the cabin, I found two things that Jason had left at the cabin—a telescope and his Bible. It was almost like he knew exactly what I needed to find my way.

"A few weeks turned into months. I sent a few photos to one of Jason's friends as a gift, not knowing she worked at a gallery. Talia tracked me down and asked for more." Dev shrugged. "It's a way to pay the electric bill and keep Violet in rawhide chews."

Jenna wasn't fooled. "You love it."

Dev didn't answer.

"You don't have to feel guilty about that, you know," Jenna said. "To love what you're doing. Where you are. Jason would have wanted that. I'm sure he…he *prayed* for that."

Dev was stunned by her perception.

"It doesn't feel…right." He had come to Mirror Lake bitter and angry. At God—and at himself. Happiness, contentment. Dev had felt as if he were being given gifts he didn't deserve.

"Because you were supposed to be miserable here."

"Yes," Dev said promptly.

"Do you think you'll ever…go back?"

"No." Dev didn't hesitate. "There's nothing there for me anymore. It sounds lame, but I know this is where I'm supposed to be. It's where I *want* to be."

The words vibrated between them.

"So. That's my story."

Now it was up to Jenna to decide what to do

with it. If the whole thing ended up on the front page of *Twin City Trends,* so be it.

"How much of this is off-the-record?"

The question cut deep. But Jenna *was* a professional.

"You can use whatever you want," he said quietly. "Jason told me that God can make something good out of our worst mistakes. Maybe someone will realize that no matter what they've done, where they've been, God hasn't turned his back on them, either."

Jenna looked up and Dev saw tears shimmering in her eyes.

"Someone already did."

Chapter Nineteen

"Come on, Aunt Jenna! We don't want to be late." Logan darted past Jenna wearing the orange life jacket he'd had on since breakfast. "We're supposed meet Dev at the boat landing at eight."

Just the thought of seeing Dev again kicked Jenna's pulse into high gear.

She'd been awake half the night, listening to the recording of their interview. Memorized the rise and fall of his voice. The affection when he talked about his younger brother. The grief that still swelled below the surface but no longer had the power to suck him under.

With God's help, Dev had made peace with his past. Started a new life. Become successful, even though he hadn't pursued it.

Dev had left Minnesota before Jenna had been hired at *Twin City Trends*. What would have happened if she'd met the *other* Dev McGuire. The wealthy, self-centered bachelor who'd been as comfortable stalking the runway of the magazine's "Bachelor of the Year" gala as he had the hallways of one of the Midwest's largest companies?

Caitlin had told her that Elaina Hammond had broken off her engagement to Dev because he wasn't the man she thought he was. But maybe the socialite had been looking for the wrong things.

It wasn't comforting to realize that like Elaina, Jenna probably would have considered him a great catch.

She scooped up her purse and saw the recorder on the table next to it. What was she supposed to do? Her plan had been to write a blog about traipsing through the woods with a wildlife photographer. Give the man some exposure, boost his sales.

Two things that Dev had no interest in.

Jenna had no doubt that Marlene would love to give readers an exclusive update on what the former *Twin City Trends* "Bachelor of the Year" was doing now.

The horn beeped once, a gentle reminder that she was taking too long. By the time Jenna reached the car, Tori and Logan were already sitting in the backseat.

Her nerves stretched a little tighter when they drove past Dev's cabin. There were no lights on...

"Did you hear me, Aunt Jenna?"

Jenna glanced in the rearview mirror and gave Logan an apologetic smile. "I'm sorry, sweetie. I'm a little distracted this morning."

"I said I packed an extra granola bar for Dev. Just in case he forgot to bring a snack."

"That was very thoughtful of you." After what Jenna had learned about Jason McGuire, she knew why Dev looked at Logan and saw his younger brother.

She wished she could have met him.

"Do you think Dev's there already?"

"We're about to find out." Jenna turned at the sign for the bed-and-breakfast. At the mailbox, a man wearing a bright yellow polo shirt and matching ball cap waved a clipboard at her.

Jenna pulled over to the side of the road and rolled down her window. Peering out, she recognized Daniel Redstone, one of Kate's friends from Church of the Pines.

"'Morning, Jenna," came the jovial greeting. "Take a few minutes to fill out this emergency contact information and turn it in to Matt before you leave," he said with a smile. "Park anywhere you see an empty spot and then head down to the lake. Sam Keller will match you up with a canoe." He turned his attention to Logan. "Do you know what the most important rule is, young man?"

Logan's eyes widened and he shook his head.

A grin split Daniel's weathered features. "Have fun."

"I like that rule." Logan grinned back.

Jenna pulled forward and scanned the line of cars, looking for an empty spot. And a black SUV.

As soon as she parked, Logan tumbled out of the backseat to greet Mulligan and Lady. Kate broke away from the group of women ladling out cold lemonade and jogged over.

"I can keep an eye on Tori while you check Logan in," she offered. "Emma and I are helping Abby put together snacks. Once we get that done, I heard we're invited to a special afternoon tea." She winked at Jenna.

"Thanks, Kate."

"No problem. That's what friends are for." Kate swung Tori up in her arms. "We'll be in the kitchen when you're ready."

"Hey, Jenna. Logan." Matthew Wilde waved a clipboard at them. "Ready to go?"

"He was ready at five o'clock this morning," Jenna told the pastor with a smile.

"I like that kind of enthusiasm." Matt took the information sheet from her and added it to the pile. "Sam? We've got another one ready to go."

To Jenna's surprise, a young woman broke away from the group and sauntered toward them. Tall and slender, she was dressed with an eye for function rather than fashion in cargo shorts and a khaki T-shirt with the words *Keller Outfitters* on the front. Her strawberry blond hair was pulled back in a high ponytail, accentuating delicate features and wide, chocolate brown eyes.

"This is Logan Gardner and his aunt, Jenna." Matt turned to Jenna. "Samantha Keller. Our official guide for the day. She learned from the best."

"My grandpa, Ben Keller." She winked at Logan. "He made the canoe you're going to be using today."

Logan's eyes lit up. "Sweet!"

Samantha laughed. "I'll give you and your partner a few pointers before we leave."

"He's not here yet."

Sam didn't miss a beat. "That gives us time to fit you with a life jacket while we wait. Head over to the boathouse—"

"I'm here."

Jenna swung around. Until that moment, she hadn't realized how afraid she'd been that Dev had changed his mind about accompanying Logan on the canoe trip.

Maybe he'd regretted telling her about Jason. Maybe he thought his personal business was about to be splashed across the pages of *Twin City Trends* so he'd packed up and moved on.

Men don't keep their promises, Jenna.

The thought had chewed at the edges of her mind as the minutes ticked by. Nola had repeated those words every time Jenna's father had walked out the door. Jenna thought she'd stopped listening to the whispers from her past but now she realized that she hadn't been completely able to silence them.

She also realized something else.

Her mother was wrong. Some men did keep their promises.

And one of those men was striding toward them, a smile on his face.

Dev saw Jenna and Logan near the waterfront, talking to Samantha Keller. Her grandfather, Ben, an avid outdoorsman and fishing guide, had offered advice when Dev had been a city boy who hadn't been able to tell the difference between a red fern and poison ivy.

Ben had suffered a mild stroke several months ago, so Sam and her son had moved in with him for the summer. If Sam had taken his place today, Dev could only assume the swift recovery they'd been hoping for hadn't taken place.

His gaze shifted to Jenna and it felt as if he were coming down with something. Dry mouth. Shortness of breath. Dev knew he had it bad.

She had taken him totally by surprise when she'd hinted that she had become a Christian.

But that didn't mean Jenna was going to stay in Mirror Lake.

He saw Sam point to the boathouse, where Jake Sutton was handing out life jackets to the boys and their mentors, and quickened his pace.

"Sorry I'm late." He couldn't take his eyes off Jenna. Her hair fell loose around her shoulders and the dress she wore accentuated her curves.

"Tori's tea party." She'd caught him staring and blushed. "She insisted we get dressed up."

Dev dragged his gaze away. "Hey, Sam."

"Dev. I'm...surprised to see you here."

He guessed that Sam was surprised to see him anywhere. Maybe he did need to get out more. He could feel the covert glances cast his way, as if he were a black bear who'd lumbered out of its cave in the middle of winter.

"I'm Logan's partner on the canoe trip."

Sam looked surprised by that, too.

The guy standing next to her stretched out a hand. "Dev McGuire?"

"That's right." Did everyone know him?

"Matt Wilde. We've talked on the phone a few times."

The pastor of the little white church in town. Matt had left messages, asking if Dev would be interested in speaking to a group of boys from single parent families. The guy wasn't nearly as tenacious as Gabby Bunker, but he hadn't given up until Dev had finally called him back and said that he "needed to keep his schedule flexible" given the nature of his work.

It had sounded good at the time.

"Nice to meet you."

"I didn't realize you were going with Logan today."

"Dev's our neighbor," Logan piped up. "He knows lots of cool stuff."

Matt tucked the clipboard under his arm, a glint in his eyes. "Like what?"

"The word is going to get out, you know," Jenna murmured. "I have a feeling that your days as Mirror Lake's favorite recluse are numbered."

So did Dev. But for once, the thought didn't send panic shooting through him. He'd been thinking about something Jenna had said. He had kept people at arm's length because he didn't think he deserved to be happy. He'd made peace with God, but in some areas, he had never made peace with himself.

Jenna had shown him that.

God puts people in your life for a reason.

All along, Dev had been thinking that God had brought Jenna and the children in his life so he could help them.

It suddenly occurred to him that maybe it was the other way around.

* * *

"That was the best tea party in the whole wide world." Abby set her empty cup down. "Mulligan and Lady and I thank you for inviting us, Tori."

Tori giggled. "You're welcome."

Lady, who wore a checkered yellow-and-white bandana around her neck, picked up her paw for Tori to shake. Mulligan, not so happy in one of Alex's ties, cast a longing look at Abby's red convertible.

"Thank you for coming." Jenna gave her an impulsive hug, which Abby returned. "It meant a lot to Tori."

"Well, it's our turn next time." Kate reached for her beaded purse. "Lucy and Ethel know how to put on a pretty fancy tea, too. We should make it a monthly event—" Kate caught herself and gave Jenna an apologetic look.

"I want your punch recipe," Abby said swiftly. "I want to serve it at the inn."

"We found it in a book." Tori took Abby's hand and led her to the kitchen.

"I'm sorry, Jenna," Kate said in a low voice. "I keep forgetting that you're going back to Minneapolis."

So did she.

"I'm glad you and Abby could come over while Logan and Dev went on the canoe trip."

Kate clipped a leash on Mulligan's collar.

"Emma and Zoey would have loved to join us, too, but they'd already volunteered to paddle the canoe with extra supplies." She tipped her head and a curl sprang free from her up do. "I still can't believe that Dev agreed to go. We've been trying for years to coax him out of his shell."

"What's your secret?" Abby, who'd tuned into the conversation, gave Jenna a wide smile.

"Dev likes us," Tori said.

"Oh, I'm sure that's true."

Jenna pretended not to see the way Kate wiggled her eyebrows at Abby. "Dev has been good for Logan."

"And you've been good for Dev." Abby tucked the recipe card in her purse and gave her a hug. "We'll see you at the cookout. The boys should be back around six."

Jenna walked them out to the car and then threw the ball for Violet a few times. The dog had been a perfect lady throughout the party, tolerating the straw hat Tori had tied on her head as she nibbled one of Abby's homemade dog biscuits.

By the time Jenna returned to the cabin, Tori was sound asleep on the sofa, her pudgy arms wrapped around her stuffed dog, Princess, the tiara set at a crooked angle on her head.

"Shhh." Jenna put a finger to her lips and Violet flopped onto the rug.

The phone rang while she was washing the

dishes and Jenna hurried to answer it before Tori woke up. "Hello?"

"Miss Gardner?"

The voice sounded vaguely familiar. "Yes. This is Jenna Gardner."

"Dr. O'Neil. I'm one of the counselors at New Day, where your sister, Shelly, had been staying."

Past tense.

Dread pooled in Jenna's stomach. "What can I do for you?"

"Your sister listed this number in her emergency contact information and I thought you should know that Shelly checked out of the treatment center early this morning."

"I talked to her several days ago and she mentioned being there at least another week."

Jenna's panic began to swell in the short silence that followed. "Shelly left without the center's support or consent. We had a session yesterday afternoon and I tried to convince Shelly to stay at least another month."

"Another *month?*"

"At New Day, we treat the whole person, not just the addiction," Dr. O'Neil said. "In my opinion, your sister still has some unresolved issues she needs to work through and it's my job to help with that. In our last session, I got the impression that Shelly was feeling…pressured…to leave."

The comment scraped against Jenna's already

raw nerves. It was so like Shelly to twist the truth. "I'm sorry if I said something to make Shelly believe that I was anxious for her to leave the center. I did take time off work, but I told her that I was happy to stay with Logan and Tori until she got back."

"I wasn't referring to you, Miss Gardner," the doctor said, a strange inflection in her tone. "Shelly left this morning and there's no question in my mind that she doesn't plan to return."

Jenna glanced at her watch. New Day was a two-hour drive from Mirror Lake. If Shelly had left early that morning, she could already be on her way.

"When she gets here, I'll do my best to convince her to go back," Jenna heard herself say, even though she knew that any influence she'd had on Shelly had disappeared long ago.

"That's one of the reasons I called you. I'm not certain that Shelly plans to return to Mirror Lake."

Jenna frowned. "Where else would she go? She knows I'm here with the Logan and Tori."

"One of the aides saw Shelly's boyfriend waiting for her in the parking lot when she checked out this morning."

"Her boyfriend?" The words sparked a rushing sound in Jenna's ears. "Who is he? Why didn't Shelly mention him before?"

"I'm afraid I'm not at liberty to discuss that

with you." Dr. O'Neil sighed, expressing her opinion that she wished it were otherwise. "I suggest you call Grace Eversea and talk to her. Although Shelly has every legal right to take her children, it may not be in Logan's and Tori's best interest to be with her...companion."

Fear that Shelly wouldn't return now took second to the fear that she *would*.

"I'm on call this weekend if you need to talk to me," Dr. O'Neil offered. "I left a message on Shelly's phone, asking her to call me. In spite of anything she might have been told to the contrary, we care about her."

The subtle reference to Shelly's boyfriend didn't exactly put Jenna at ease.

Somehow, she had to get in touch with Dev. His cell phone went right to voice mail, which meant that he'd either turned it off or they'd drifted out of signal range.

God, Dev said that you don't abandon your children during the storms. I trust that you're here and that you're watching over us.

An unexpected peace swept through Jenna.

Maybe Dev was right. Maybe she didn't have to do this alone.

Chapter Twenty

Dev pulled the canoe onto shore and scanned the faces of the people walking to the shoreline to greet the boys upon their return.

"Do you see your aunt?"

Logan looked around and shook his head. "Maybe she's inside."

"How about you take the life jackets back and I'll look around for her?" Dev slipped his off and handed it to Logan.

They'd been scheduled to return well over an hour ago, but one of the boys had wandered off while everyone was eating lunch, forcing Sam Keller and Matt to organize an impromptu search party. The boy had eventually been found, sound asleep in the shade of an oak tree, a half-eaten peanut butter sandwich in his hand.

Other than that, the afternoon had drifted by without a hitch. Logan had loved the trip, talking a mile a minute and pointing out everything he saw, from a bald eagle perched in the branches of a jack pine to a painted turtle sunning itself on a log.

Paddling through a narrow channel, Dev had found himself wondering if Jenna would be glad to put the past few weeks behind her when she returned to the city. The pace might be slower here but she had been under a tremendous amount of pressure because of the situation with her sister.

Dev was just as concerned as she was about Logan and Tori. They needed stability. Someone to look after them and nurture their dreams. Jenna doubted her ability, but Dev knew she'd be good at both.

He made his way over to the grill where Abby stood, spatula in hand as she lined up burgers on a metal grate over the coals.

"Do you know where Jenna is?"

"She hasn't shown up yet." Abby smiled. "Tori was pretty wiped out from all the excitement. Maybe she took a long nap."

"Maybe." Dev couldn't imagine that Jenna wouldn't have given them a heads-up that she would be late. He'd left his cell in the glove compartment so it was possible she'd left a voice mail. "Can you tell Logan I'll be right back?"

"Will do."

Dev didn't miss the smile that passed between Abby and Kate. No doubt about it. The cloak of mystery he'd worn was becoming more transparent by the hour.

He checked his phone and felt a stab of unease. Three missed calls and a text message.

Please bring Logan home ASAP.

Lord, I don't know what's going on but you do. Take care of Jenna. Let her know that whatever is happening, you're right there with her.

"Did Jenna leave a…" Kate's smile faded. "What's wrong?"

"She wants me to bring Logan home. Right away."

"He's over there, with Jeremy and Cody." Kate pointed to a group of boys playing Frisbee.

"Did something happen?" Abby asked.

"I'm not sure."

"What can we do?"

"Pray." Dev tossed the word over his shoulder as he went to get Logan.

The drive seemed to take twice as long as usual. Dev pulled up close to the cabin and hopped out. Jenna met him on the porch.

"Where's Logan?" Panic flared in her eyes.

"In the backseat. He fell asleep on the way home." Dev pivoted toward his car. "I'll be right back, and then we'll talk."

It worried him that Jenna didn't argue. The

bleak look in her eyes told Dev this was something more serious than a newspaper article or unearthing information about his past.

Jenna was still at the door when he returned with Logan in his arms. When she reached for him, Dev shook his head.

"I'll help."

Jenna didn't argue about that, either.

Logan woke up long enough to change into his pajamas and crawl into bed. When Dev would have closed the door behind them, Jenna put out a hand to stop him.

"Leave it open. Please." Her voice shook.

"Tell me what happened."

Haltingly, Jenna told him about the phone call she'd received from Shelly's counselor at the treatment center.

"And you haven't heard from her yet?"

"I tried to call her cell phone a few times but she didn't answer."

"You think she's on her way here?"

"I have no idea." Jenna glanced over her shoulder, making sure the children hadn't woken up and wandered out of the bedroom. "Dr. O'Neil said that she left with a man. Her boyfriend."

"I take it that you didn't know about him?"

"No." Jenna sounded bitter. "It's not like Shelly confided in me. Dr. O'Neil couldn't say much without breaking confidentiality rules, but she alluded to the fact that he might not be a…safe…person for the children to be with."

And this person, whoever he was, could show up at the door any minute. Legally, Jenna had no authority to prevent her sister from taking control of her children again.

Dev thought about the guy in black that he'd caught hanging around in the woods.

"Violet and I will camp out on the porch tonight. There's no way I'm leaving you and the kids alone." Jenna opened her mouth and Dev put his finger against her lips. "Don't try to talk me out of it."

Jenna smiled for the first time.

"I was going to say thank you."

A low growl roused Jenna from a fitful sleep.

She sat bolt upright in bed next to Tori, blinking to dispel the darkness. A shadow blotted out the crease of light under the door.

Jenna prayed it was Dev.

Careful not to disturb Tori, she slid out of bed and peered into the living room.

A beam of moonlight clearly defined Violet's silhouette in the middle of the room, her ears at high alert, an uneven ridge of fur bristling down her spine.

Jenna took a step forward and suddenly Dev was there, a solid, comforting presence beside her.

"Violet heard something," she whispered.

"There's a car coming down the driveway." Dev's hand closed around hers for a moment, offering his strength. "Wait here." The floor creaked as he padded to the front door.

Jenna felt a cold nose press against her leg. She reached down to pat Violet, who growled again as the soft but unmistakable snick of a car door closing disrupted the silence.

The few times Jenna had allowed herself to dream of reuniting with Shelly, this was far from the scenario she'd pictured in her mind.

Jenna's heart thumped in response to a soft tap on the door.

"I need to speak with Jenna."

Jenna recognized the voice immediately and fear distilled into a cold, mind-numbing dread. She took a jerky step out of the shadows as Dev flipped on the porch light, illuminating the man framed in the doorway.

Jake Sutton might have been wearing jeans and a T-shirt but the grim expression on his face relayed the fact that he was there on official business.

And other than a brief measuring look, the police chief didn't look surprised to find Dev standing guard at the door. His attention shifted to her.

"May I come in?"

Jenna managed a jerky nod. "W-what happened? Did Shelly ask you to pick up Logan and Tori?"

She wouldn't put it past Shelly to ask the police to pick up the children for her, neatly bypassing any questions Jenna might have about her decision to leave New Day.

Jake glanced at the bedroom door, where the children were sleeping. "Maybe you should sit down," he suggested quietly.

Jenna's lips parted but no sound came out. Dev was at her side in an instant. He slipped an arm around her waist and pulled her close, absorbed the tremor that rattled through her.

"It'll be okay." Dev guided her to the kitchen table and pulled out a chair.

Jake followed them but remained standing. "Shelly didn't ask me to come here. She and her companion were pulled over by a sheriff's deputy several hours ago.

"They attempted to flee the scene, but the driver lost control of the vehicle and ran into a fence. They weren't seriously injured," he added quickly. "Just a few minor bumps and bruises."

Jenna was thankful for that but instinctively knew there was more to the story.

"Where is Shelly now?"

Sutton hesitated a fraction of a second.

"When the officers searched the car, they found illegal narcotics. Enough that both Shelly and her boyfriend were arrested for possession and intent to deliver."

"She never mentioned a boyfriend." Jenna caught her lower lip between her teeth. "Neither did Logan or Tori."

"Owen Radley." Jake glanced at Dev. "He fit the description of the guy you saw hanging around last week. When I questioned him, he said he didn't realize Jenna was staying here with the kids. He wanted a place to crash for a night or two, but changed his mind when you confronted him."

"You *talked* to him?" Jenna stared at Dev. "Why didn't you say anything?"

"I didn't want to worry you." Dev raked a hand through his hair. "I just figured I'd keep a close eye on things over here. I planned to let Jake know if the guy showed up again, but he never came back."

Because he'd found Shelly.

"I don't understand," Jenna whispered. "The last time I talked to my sister, she said the treatment was going well."

Jake's expression softened. "I'm sorry, Jenna."

"What happens now? When will she get out of jail?"

"Your sister had a prior conviction last summer so she was already on probation for shoplifting and resisting arrest," Jake explained carefully. "With the added charges from tonight, I'm afraid she could be facing some prison time."

Jenna flinched.

Dev asked the question that she couldn't. "How long?"

"If the judge is lenient, my guess would be three to five years."

Three to five years.

The ramifications weren't lost on either of them. Even if the sentence were reduced, Shelly would miss out on a significant portion of Logan's and Tori's childhood.

"What about the children?" Jenna heard her voice crack and Dev reached for her hand, sharing his strength.

"I called Grace. She's going to come over first thing in the morning and talk to you." Jake sighed. "I don't enjoy this part of my job, but I thought the words might be easier coming from a friend."

"Thank you. I appreciate that."

Jake paused at the door. "Jenna?" He waited until she looked up. "Emma and I…we'll be praying for you and the kids."

"Will you…will you pray for Shelly, too?"

Admiration flickered in the police chief's eyes. "We certainly will."

"I'll put a pot of coffee on."

Dev knew that neither one of them would be able to fall back to sleep.

"I have no idea how I'm going to tell Logan and

Tori." Jenna wrapped her arms around her middle, as if that were the only thing holding her together at the moment.

"I'm sure that Grace will do whatever she can to help you."

Dev had never felt so helpless. He wanted to fix everything. Bear the weight of Jenna's pain.

He doubted that she had considered the possibility that Shelly might not make it through the treatment program. Dev certainly hadn't.

"Prison, Dev. Shelly could be going to prison." Jenna shook her head. "Over the past few days, I'd been thinking that I should find a house in town for them to rent. Ask Kate if she had an opening at the cafe for a full-time waitress. I know she'd be willing to work around Logan's and Tori's school day. I figured if Shelly got to know the people here, she'd fall in love with them. With Mirror Lake. This could be home, if she'd give it a chance."

It could be your home, too.

Dev didn't say the words out loud. Jenna's life— her career—were in Minneapolis. Those things hadn't changed, even if his feelings for her had.

The snap of a car door brought them to their feet. Dev looked out the window and saw Kate's vintage Thunderbird. Grace Eversea was getting out of the passenger side of the vehicle.

Jenna stepped onto the porch to meet them. "I'm glad you're here."

Kate hugged her. "Grace called and told me what happened to Shelly. I'm so sorry."

"So am I." Jenna's eyes misted over. "Logan and Tori have been through so much already."

Grace joined them. "Can we talk in private for a few minutes, Jenna?"

Dev let out a breath. "I can come back later."

"Please. Stay," Jenna murmured.

She didn't have to ask him twice.

They sat down on the porch and Jenna turned to Grace.

"I hope you can give me some advice on how to make the transition easier for them. Finding out their mom isn't coming back is going to be hard enough, but the move—"

Grace put her hand on Jenna's arm. "I talked to Shelly this morning. She wants Logan and Tori to stay in Mirror Lake."

"For how long?" Jenna frowned. "At some point, I have to go back to Minneapolis and the children will be starting school in a few weeks. There are a lot of plans to make."

"Jenna—" Grace glanced at Kate. "Shelly requested that Logan and Tori be placed in foster care again."

Chapter Twenty-One

"Foster care." Jenna felt the ground shift below her feet. "Shelly wanted me to take the children after the fire. Why would she change her mind?"

"She didn't explain," Grace said. "She asked me to make other arrangements as soon as possible."

Other arrangements.

The lump in Jenna's throat swelled as her gaze swung to Kate. "That's why you're here."

"I'm here because I'm your friend," Kate said swiftly. "And because I love Logan and Tori. We're going to figure this out together."

Grace gave Jenna's arm a comforting squeeze. "I'm going to set up a meeting with my director. The court does take the parent's wishes into consideration, but I believe we can make a strong case for the fact that the children should remain with you for the time being. Until you decide what you want to do."

"Thank you." A few weeks ago, Jenna had hoped that caring for her niece and nephew would be a temporary arrangement. Now she didn't want to lose them.

"I'll be in touch," Grace promised.

"And I'll be praying." Kate took Jenna by the hands. "This didn't take God by surprise. He's in control and he loves you. Don't ever forget that."

Jenna nodded, unable to trust her voice.

The car rattled down the driveway and only years of hiding her feelings kept Jenna from losing it.

Dev took a step closer but Jenna stumbled away. "Dev...I want to be alone."

"A few minutes ago you said that I could stay."

Jenna tried to smile. "In about five seconds I'm going to fall to pieces—" She gasped when Dev's arms slipped around her waist. Drew her close. His lips brushed the sensitive spot below her ear.

"Then I'll catch you."

Dev absorbed the tremor that shook Jenna's slender frame. Soothed her with quiet words. Waited for the storm to pass.

He didn't know what to do with his feelings for Jenna, but he couldn't deny them anymore.

"It'll be okay." Dev would do everything in his power to make sure of it.

"What do I do now?" Jenna spoke so softly that

Dev had to strain to hear the words. "Shelly doesn't want Logan and Tori to live with me."

"What do *you* want?"

"To stay together."

She's talking about the children.

Dev sent the ruthless reminder to intercept the hope that arrowed through him.

"Ask Jake Sutton if you can meet with Shelly," he told her. "Find out what she's thinking."

"Do you think she'll agree to see me?" Hope and doubt battled for control. "Shelly can be stubborn. Once she makes up her mind about something, it's almost impossible to change it."

"Talk to your sister." Dev stepped back, tucked a strand of hair behind Jenna's ear. "I'll take Logan and Tori over to Kate's after breakfast."

"All right."

But instead of walking away, Jenna went up on her toes and pressed her palms against his chest. Brushed a kiss against his lips that wrapped around his heart—twice—and took it captive.

"Thank you," she whispered.

And then she walked away, taking it with her.

"Hey, sis. How's it going?"

If Jenna had passed her sister on the street, she wouldn't have recognized her. The long, platinum blond hair that Shelly had spent hours fussing over as a teenager had been shorn almost down to the scalp, each spike tipped in black. Big blue eyes that had once sparkled with life stared back at her, bleak and world-weary.

"Hi." Jenna wanted nothing more than to wrap her arms around her sister and hold her tight, but Shelly's brittle smile warned her not to.

"You look good." Shelly leaned back in the metal folding chair and crossed her arms. "Just like your picture in the magazine. Now my picture…" She touched the purplish bruise on her cheek. "I'm pretty sure that will only make it as far as the police department's central database."

Jenna couldn't believe she was cracking jokes. "I'm sorry."

"I'm sure you are. Sorry that I disappointed you. You probably thought you didn't have to think about me ever again."

"That isn't true. I've never stopped thinking about you. You're my sister. I care about you."

Something flickered in Shelly's eyes. "Well, right now you're the only one that does. Owen told the cops the drugs were mine. I didn't even know he had them. He said he wanted me to take a little road trip with him. It was Vance all over again."

Her lips twisted in a parody of a smile. "This is the part where you get to say I told you so."

"I wanted you to be happy. I wanted Vance to be good to you and Logan."

"So did I." Shelly shrugged. "I traveled with

the band for a while, but after I got pregnant with Tori, I gave him an ultimatum. The band or us. I'm sure you can guess what he chose. I haven't seen him for a couple of years. Heard he married some groupie."

"Tori and Logan never mentioned that you were with someone else now," Jenna said cautiously.

"They'd never met Owen. We hung out at a concert a few months ago. He made a lot of promises. The house, the white picket fence. I packed up the kids and followed him to Mirror Lake. Only he wasn't here—and you saw the house. Turns out he didn't even own it."

"You should have called me."

"And mess up your perfect life? I figured you were better off not having to worry about me and I was right."

"I don't have a perfect life."

"Oh, please. I've read your column."

Shelly had read only what Jenna had been brave enough to reveal. She never talked about her past. Unlike Dev, she'd never considered that some of her readers might be able to relate to her mistakes as well as her successes.

God, there's been seven years of silence. I don't know how to close the gap between us.

Jenna twisted a finger around the piece of yarn that circled her wrist.

Shelly spotted it and leaned forward, drawing a frown from the guard who stood near the door.

"Did Tori make that for you?"

When Jenna nodded, Shelly rolled back the sleeve of her orange jumpsuit. On her wrist was a bracelet identical to the one Jenna wore. "She loves pink."

All Jenna could do was nod. She'd prayed for a connection with Shelly and here it was. A piece of string braided together by a little girl.

Tears banked behind her eyes.

Thank you, God.

"Tori and Logan...they're great kids."

"No thanks to me. I tried to keep up with them, but I got so tired. I just wanted to forget everything." Shelly's fingers tapped against the table, pinching a cigarette that wasn't there. "The pills helped with that. Whenever they wore off, the pain came back. I guess I'm just like Mom. You're the one who got it right."

"No, I didn't." Jenna took a chance and reached out to take her sister's hand. "I was missing the most important thing."

"You met someone."

Jenna smiled. "You could say that. I didn't realize a person could have a personal relationship with God. I didn't think I could trust him because I couldn't trust anyone else."

"You can't." Shelly pulled away. "Everyone

breaks their promises. Even me. I told you things would be different and look where I am."

"You're right. People will let us down but God won't. For years, I was afraid to count on anyone. I didn't want to be disappointed again."

"Yeah, Mom was good at that." Shelly slumped down in the chair. "Mom dumped everything on you—including me. I knew that once you got that scholarship, you were going to go places. I didn't want to hold you back then and I'm not going to do it now. I know what you sacrificed for me when we were growing up."

Jenna stared at her sister in disbelief. Had that been the basis for Shelly's decision to place the children back in foster care? A few minutes ago, she'd said something about messing up Jenna's "perfect life."

A lump swelled in her throat. "Is that why you don't want me to take care of Logan and Tori?"

"I can't ask you to raise my kids, Jenna. Not when you had to raise me."

"You don't have to ask me." Jenna reached out and took Shelly's hand. "I'm asking *you*. Please let Tori and Logan live with me."

Shelly looked at her with cautious hope. "You want them?"

"Yes." Jenna's vision blurred. She was glad she'd taken Dev's advice and met with her sister.

"They're my family. I can't promise that I'll always do everything right but I...I'll love them."

"I know you will." For the first time, Shelly's smile was genuine and Jenna saw a glimpse of the sister she remembered. "You were always good at that, too."

Dev had alternated between pacing and praying the remainder of the afternoon. He'd finally walked down to the dock, hoping the familiar, soothing sound of the water would calm his restless thoughts. When Jenna finally did return, Dev was so deep in thought he didn't see her until she was standing beside him.

"The kids?"

"They're still with Kate. I stopped here first."

Dev tried not to read too much into that. Jenna would need time to process what had to have been an emotional reunion with her sister.

Jenna kicked off her shoes and dragged a toe through the water. "Shelly agreed to let me to take Logan and Tori back to Minneapolis with me."

"That's what you wanted."

"I know." Jenna looked as if she could hardly believe Shelly had changed her mind. "She wants to give me full custody. Even when she gets out of prison, Logan and Tori will stay with me. I'm going to be *raising* them."

Dev heard a thread of panic in Jenna's voice.

"And you'll do a great job," he said quietly. "You love Tori and Logan—and they love you."

"They love it here. I don't know how they'll feel about moving to Minneapolis with me."

Then stay here, Dev wanted to say. But he dug deep to give Jenna the encouragement she needed.

"It will be an adjustment but you'll be together."

Jenna began to pace, unwittingly following the same path he'd worn in the sand. "How am I supposed to help Logan with his math? I can barely balance my checkbook. And Tori. I don't know how to sew—"

"Whoa. You lost me."

"Costumes." Jenna saw his blank look. "For school plays. What if she has to be a pilgrim or a tree or—"

"I think you're getting a little ahead of yourself." Dev tried not to smile.

"That's easy for you to say. This isn't temporary, Dev. This isn't being Aunt Jenna for a holiday or a long weekend."

"You can do it. You've been doing it," he felt the need to remind her. "Everything Logan and Tori need, you've been providing the past few weeks. And God will give you what *you* need."

"Are you sure?"

"He promised."

Jenna drew a shaky breath. Smiled. "Okay. I'm

going to drive over to the inn and pick them up. Grace wants to meet with us after that."

She didn't ask him to go along. But she did reach out and take his hand.

"Thank you."

Dev watched Jenna run toward the car, barefoot.

Good job, Dev.

He'd just talked the woman he loved into leaving.

Chapter Twenty-Two

"A letter from an adoring reader?"

Jenna smiled up at Caitlin, who'd called earlier that morning and invited her out to lunch.

"A *disgruntled* reader," she corrected. "My in-box is full of them. No one wants to know how to accessorize for fall. Everyone wants to hear more about Mirror Lake."

"I don't blame them. I want to hear more about Mirror Lake, too." Caitlin propped her hip against the side of Jenna's desk. "Especially Hank the chainsaw artist. He is quite the charmer."

Jenna focused on the computer screen. Much easier than the knowing look in her friend's eyes.

"Hank loves the attention."

"Unlike *some* people, who shall remain nameless." Caitlin's lips curved in a slow smile. "Thanks to you."

"Hank was—" *Second* "—on Gabby's list."

"I suppose you're going to say that it's all about giving the readers what they want."

Jenna tried not to smile back. "Yes, it is."

And scrapping Dev's interview for the *Mirror Lake Register* was the only way she could be certain that his name would never appear in *Twin City Trends*.

Dev had trusted her. Not only with his past, but in some respects, his future, too. Jenna didn't want someone like Dawn Gallagher putting her own spin on things. She'd decided that if Dev ever decided to tell his story, his name would be on the byline.

Fortunately, Gabby had agreed with her.

"We take care of our own in Mirror Lake," the elderly reporter had proclaimed after Jenna played the recording of their interview. "And Dev McGuire is *our* recluse. I say we keep it that way."

Jenna had hugged her. "Thank you."

Gabby had looked at her shrewdly. "When are you going to tell Dev that you changed your mind about writing the article?"

"He'll find out when he reads next week's paper."

A going-away gift.

Jenna wondered what Dev had thought when he'd found the newspaper in his mailbox. Had he been surprised? Relieved? It had taken every ounce of her self-control not to call him and find out.

"I heard a rumor downstairs that Hank might

take part in the bachelor auction this spring," Caitlin said as they walked together toward the elevator.

"Marlene wants me to head up the committee, but I suggested she ask Dawn instead. Logan and Tori keep me pretty busy."

A better kind of busy.

"How are they doing?"

"They start school next week. There's a three-bedroom unit opening up in my apartment complex soon, so that's good."

Caitlin gave her a sideways glance. "Is it?"

"Sure. We need the extra space. Tori bought a goldfish at the pet store last weekend." And named him Fred the Second. "Logan found out there's a science club at the school he'll be attending."

"And how are *you* doing?"

Jenna sighed. "I went to the gallery yesterday and bought one of Dev's photographs."

A night sky. Just to feel closer to him.

"That's what I thought."

Jenna saw the smug look on Caitlin's face and groaned. "I couldn't wait to get back here and now something is...missing."

"Dev."

"I'm pathetic." Jenna punched the button for the first floor with more force than necessary.

"You're in love."

Jenna couldn't deny it. "I can't expect Dev to come back to the city. I wouldn't want him to."

"And you certainly wouldn't want to move to Mirror Lake." Caitlin shuddered. "Small towns. Everyone knows everyone else's business."

Jenna didn't think that was a fair statement. "The people keep an eye on each other but it's because they care."

"And look at everything you'd have to give up. I feel sorry for Abby O'Halloran. She must be experiencing a severe case of culture shock after living in Chicago."

"Abby loves Mirror Lake," Jenna protested. "Her bed-and-breakfast is doing well and Alex plans to move there by Christmas. I don't think she misses the city at all…" Jenna stopped. "You are so *sneaky*."

Caitlin didn't look the least bit repentant. "I have a teenage daughter, twin boys, a dog and an iguana. It comes with the territory."

"My boss would never agree to let me write my column from Mirror Lake."

Caitlin raised an eyebrow. "All those emails in your in-box tell me otherwise."

Jenna ignored the tiny seed of hope that tried to take root. "I can't be City Girl in Mirror Lake."

"But you can be Jenna. Writing about the ups and downs that all of us experience—only you'll be the one brave enough to write them down." Caitlin smiled. "And you can do that anywhere. In your car while you wait for the last bell to ring at Logan and Tori's school. On a park bench while they play…even on a dock overlooking a cute little lake with a handsome wildlife photographer at your side."

"What if—" Jenna stopped, afraid to voice her deepest fear.

"Dev doesn't feel the same way about you."

"He didn't even try to talk me out of going back to Minneapolis."

"Did you try to talk him into coming here?"

"No." Jenna was shocked her friend could even suggest such a thing. "Dev's life is in Mirror Lake. He loves it there. I would never ask him to do that because I—"

"Love him."

"I didn't say that!"

"You didn't have to." Caitlin smiled. "So…"

"So, what?"

"If you would never ask Dev to leave Mirror Lake because you love him, doesn't it make sense that he didn't ask you to stay for the very same reason?"

Violet leaped over Dev in her haste to get out of the vehicle.

"Sorry I'm not moving fast enough for you," he called.

The dog didn't look the least bit guilty as she loped toward the trees, a clear destination in mind.

"Violet, no—" Dev gave up and let her go.

He'd stretched out his latest shoot an extra two days before he realized there was no point in postponing the inevitable. He had to come home sometime, and when he did, Jenna and the kids wouldn't be there.

He just hadn't expected the place to feel so empty. *He* hadn't expected to feel so empty.

Dev tried to tell himself that it was for the best. Jenna's best. Her career was based in the city. Logan and Tori would have access to a private school and all the perks of living in an urban area.

He wasn't naive enough to think everyone had to relocate to a cabin in the woods to find peace.

Dev slung the camera bag over his shoulder and felt his muscles protest. He was getting too old to sleep on the ground.

His cell phone rang and when Dev saw Talia's number come up on the tiny screen, he rolled his eyes. Did she have him under surveillance? How did she know that he'd just gotten home?

"Hi, Talia. Yes, I have some pictures for you."

"That's good news but it's not why I called."

"Really?" Dev looked around for Violet. "You called to convince me to reprint some of my photographs?"

"I called to tell you that one of your photographs sold a few days ago."

"Which one?" Dev asked, not out of curiosity but because it was expected of him.

"Psalm 19."

"No way." Dev groaned.

"That wasn't the reaction I was hoping for."

"I was going to ask you to pull that one."

"What?"

Dev had somehow managed the impossible. He'd shocked Talia Hunt.

"Dev, it's one of your best ones."

"I was going to give it to a friend."

"You're making friends? I'm so proud of you."

"That would be Jenna's fault." Dev had been getting invites over for supper. Church outings. A woman with a pink cane had even shown up at his door with a casserole the day before he'd left.

"Who's Jenna?"

Had he really said her name out loud? That showed his head wasn't in the game. "I should go, Talia. Violet took off."

"That excuse is like a Get Out of Jail Free card. You can only use it once. I repeat. Who's Jenna?"

"My next door neighbor." But not anymore.

"That's strange. Because the woman who bought Psalm 19 said that her name was Jenna. Jenna Gardner."

Dev's duffle bag dropped to the dirt at his feet.

"You *met* Jenna?"

"We had coffee together. She's great. Pretty, too. Now what were you saying about photographs?"

"I take them."

Talia burst out laughing. "I know you do, sweetheart. And to give you fair warning, I'm planning to drive over at the end of the week to pick them up."

Jenna had bought one of his photographs. One he'd taken several months ago of the night sky.

He had to find out why.

"Don't you dare."

"Dev—"

"I'll bring them to you."

Another first. Talia speechless. "When?"

Dev glanced at his watch. "In about four hours."

"But—"

He hung up. Tossed the duffle bag back inside the vehicle. If he left now, he could be in Minneapolis by sunset.

"Violet!"

No response. He really had to look into obedience school.

"Road trip!"

If those two words didn't bring the dog crashing through the underbrush, nothing would.

Sure enough, a few seconds later he heard branches snapping. Violet bound out of the woods but she wasn't alone. A chubby golden retriever puppy was ambling along behind her.

Violet tossed her head, looking extremely proud of her find.

"Sorry, you can't keep her." Dev knelt down and the puppy vaulted into his lap, its entire body set in motion by the frantic wave of its tail. Bright-eyed and well-fed, it was obvious the animal wasn't a stray but it didn't have a collar or identification tags.

"You have to belong to someone—" Dev's smile faded when he looked up and saw Jenna walking toward him.

He rose slowly to his feet, dimly aware that the puppy was playing tug-of-war with the laces on his hiking boots.

"I see you met Daisy."

"Dev!" Logan and Tori burst through the trees and barreled toward him.

"Do you like Daisy?" Tori tugged on his arm. "We picked her out yesterday—"

"She's going to be as big as Violet when she's all grown up."

Dev glanced at the puppy's saucerlike feet. "You're probably right about that."

"Can we see if she likes the water, Aunt Jenna?"

Jenna laughed. "Go ahead."

Dev wanted to pinch himself to make sure he wasn't dreaming. Jenna. Here. When he'd been all set to jump in the car and go to her.

Jenna had a speech rehearsed. Practiced it in

her mind on the long car ride from Minneapolis to Mirror Lake. But now, with Dev standing three feet away, she couldn't remember a single word.

He didn't appear to know what to say, either, as he watched Daisy and Violet romp with the children in the shallow water.

"How are they adjusting?"

"They miss you," Jenna said simply.

Dev slanted a look at her. "I'm sorry. I know you were afraid of what would happen if they got too attached."

"I think," Jenna said slowly. "That I was the one afraid of getting too attached. After I talked to Shelly, I realized that we weren't so different. We both had scars from the past, but I did a better job covering them up with Vera Wang."

Dev almost smiled. "Some of us prefer flannel."

This was the man she'd fallen in love with. The one who knew what was important. The one who had fixed his eyes on the One who didn't change.

Jenna had seen the other one in the glossy pages of a few back issues of *Twin City Trends*. The Devlin McGuire who had once been on the other side of the camera.

She liked this one better. No, she *loved* this one.

Daisy barked at Violet, who lowered her ears and pretended to be intimidated.

"She looks like a handful."

"She is but we love her to pieces."

"I didn't think your condo allowed pets."

"It doesn't." Jenna fell into step with him as they walked down to the lake. "We moved."

"I suppose you needed more room."

Jenna smiled. "A wise man once told me that kids need a lot of space. That's why we came back here."

Several more steps. And then Dev stopped. Slowly turned to face her.

"You're moving here? To Mirror Lake?"

Jenna nodded, not taking her eyes from his face. "Yes."

The golden eyes darkened as if he didn't believe her. "For how long?"

"I was thinking…forever? Or as long as you're here."

Dev slowly drew her into his arms, bent his head until their lips were about to touch. The love in his eyes took her breath away.

"What do you know? I was thinking the exact same thing."

And then he kissed her. A sweet, searching kiss that took Jenna's breath away and made her believe in promises again.

Epilogue

"Hold still!"

Kate shot Jenna a stern look as she wound a checkered wool scarf around her neck and tucked it in place.

"I don't have a choice," Jenna grumbled. "I have more layers than Delia Peake's Jell-O salad."

Abby chuckled. "We don't want you to get cold on your very first winter hike."

"You know, I'm not sure those two words go together."

The front door opened and Zoey swept in with a gust of chilly November air, simultaneously stomping the snow from her boots and shaking the snowflakes from her hair.

"Sorry I'm late. I had a couple of last-minute errands to run."

"I think she's all set." Kate flicked the red pom-pom on Jenna's borrowed stocking cap over her shoulder. "Only one more thing and we're good to go."

"One more thing?"

Zoey held up a pair of snowshoes.

"I can't wear those," Jenna gasped.

Abby looked at Kate. "Didn't someone once write that in the right pair of shoes, and I believe this is a direct quote, 'a girl can go anywhere'?"

Kate tapped her jaw thoughtfully with the tip of her finger. "As a matter of fact, I do remember reading that somewhere."

"I don't think I want to venture to the places these kind of shoes are going to take me."

"Of course you do," Zoey said cheerfully.

"You're going to have fun." Emma patted her arm.

"Of course she is." Kate tossed on her coat. "She's with us!"

Jenna appreciated what her friends were doing. Dev had left for a shoot three days ago, and Jenna already felt the hole his absence had created. She thought she'd been hiding it well until Abby had called to invite her and the kids over for hot chocolate in the library.

Jenna had been ambushed on the moment of her arrival. Alex had kidnapped the children right in front of her very eyes and took them to a sledding hill on the edge of town.

Abby and Kate had been lying in wait for her

inside. Abby had made hot chocolate. But they weren't going to drink it until they returned from a long walk in the woods.

"Come on, city girl." Zoey tossed Jenna a wink and a pair of mittens. "Show them what you've got."

"At the end of the day, I guarantee you'll have something to brag about. Or..." Kate said, grinning "...blog about."

Groaning, Jenna sat down on the bottom step and reached for a snowshoe. "Let's get this over with."

They stepped out the back door of the inn and the drop in temperature snatched the breath from Jenna's lungs. An early snow had blanketed the yard and dusted the trees like powdered sugar.

"Come on." Kate set out briskly, as if she'd been born with a pair of snowshoes on her feet. "We don't want to be late."

"Late for what?"

Abby passed her up with a smile. "For the hot chocolate we promised you."

The four dogs ambled beside them, Violet barking encouragement to Daisy as they bound through the snow.

They blazed their own trail around the lake, their breath coming out in puffs of frost. Jenna forgot about her cold toes and began to appreciate the beauty of their surroundings.

"Is that smoke?" Jenna pointed to the sky.

"Could be. Maybe we should check it out."

Jenna increased her pace. It looked as if a gray cloud was close to Dev's cabin.

She missed living next door to him. They'd rented a cute little house right next door to Gabby Bunker. As much as Jenna had grown to love the cabin, it wasn't well insulated and Dev had warned her that the road could be treacherous in the winter. Now Logan and Tori were within walking distance of the elementary school.

"It's probably a campfire," Kate said. "No need to get excited."

"In the winter?"

"Hey, some people like to be outside. Look at us!"

Jenna increased her pace anyway, feeling the pull of muscles she hadn't known existed. She recognized the trail they were on now. It was the one Dev had taken her and the children on the night of their "field trip."

She reached the top of the rise and saw a familiar figure standing next to, of all things, a campfire. A smile spread across Jenna's face.

"Did you guys plan this?"

"Sorry, we can't take the credit." Kate nudged her toward Dev. "This time."

"We only did what we were told," Abby added.

"What's going on?"

"We promised you hot chocolate at the end of our hike."

"We just didn't specify where." Emma grinned.

"Or with who," Zoey added.

Laughing, the four women linked arms and trudged back down the trail.

"My partners in crime." Dev grinned. "Abby and Kate packed us enough food for an army."

"A picnic? In the snow?" Jenna grinned back. "I love it." She chucked her mittens aside and plopped down on the blanket to work at the buckles on her snowshoes. "I didn't know you were coming back today. Didn't you get the photographs you were hoping for?"

"No, but I got something else."

"Frostbite?" Jenna teased.

Dev knelt down but didn't pull off her other snowshoe. He took a small velvet box out of his pocket.

"This."

Jenna's breath knotted in her lungs when he opened it to reveal a stunning, heart-shaped diamond. On each side of it were two sapphires. Tori's and Logan's birthstone.

"I love you, Jenna. Be my wife. I want to spend the rest of my life with you. I want to be there when Logan starts to drive and intimidate the first boy that dares to ask Tori out on a date. I want to watch our little boy or girl take their first steps. I might not have all that much to offer a city girl—"

"Stop right there." Jenna pressed a finger to his lips. "I'm not a city girl anymore."

"What are you then?" Laughter danced in Dev's eyes.

Jenna slid the ring on her finger, lifted her face for his kiss.

"Yours."

* * * * *

Dear Reader,

Welcome back to Mirror Lake! I hope you enjoyed your visit!

In *The Promise of Home* Dev's heart was stirred by God's creation. And in the North Star, Jenna saw a beautiful picture of his faithfulness. God never changes—you can trust him!

I live in the country, so every time I take a walk on the trails through our woods, I think of Psalm 19. *"The heavens declared the glory of God; the skies proclaim the work of his hands."* I encourage you to read the whole chapter when you have a chance.

I have been having a lot of fun writing this series and I hope you schedule another visit to Mirror Lake soon, to reconnect with old "friends" and make new ones. Please visit my website at kathrynspringer.com and say hello. I'd love to hear from you!

Keep smiling and seeking him!

Kathryn Springer

Questions for Discussion

1. What brought Jenna to Mirror Lake? Have you ever had to drop everything to help out a family member or friend in need? Describe how you felt about it.

2. How did Jenna's childhood mirror Logan's and Tori's? Do you think that made it easier or more difficult for her to care for them?

3. What misconceptions did Dev have about Jenna when they met? Why?

4. Why didn't Jenna want Logan to get attached to Violet and Dev? What was the real reason behind her reluctance? What part did her past play in that decision?

5. Kate and her friends held a surprise "housewarming" party for Jenna. Has anyone ever done something like that for you? What was it? How did it make you feel?

6. If you could interview someone for a newspaper, who would it be? Why?

7. What was the turning point in Dev's and Jenna's relationship?